PRAISE FOR THE NOVELS OF
TARA TAYLOR QUINN

"Quinn's latest contemporary romance offers readers an irresistible combination of realistically complex characters and a nail-bitingly suspenseful plot. Powerful, passionate and poignant, *Hidden* is a deeply satisfying story."
—*Booklist*

"*Somebody's Baby* is an exceptional tale of real-life people, who are not perfect, feel heartache, make mistakes and have to find their inner strength.... *Somebody's Baby* easily goes on my keeper shelf."
—*The Romance Reader Reviews*

"Quinn explores relationships thoroughly, getting into the nooks and crannies, into the dark corners and secret cupboards. Her vividly drawn characters are sure to win readers' hearts."
—*Romance Communications*

"Quinn's profound observations of human nature and her intimate understanding of values and priorities lend extraordinary psychological depth to all her work."
—*Wordweaving.com*

"Quinn writes touching stories about real people that transcend plot type or genre."
—*All About Romance*

Dear Reader,

Happy holidays! It's been a while since I celebrated the season, my favorite time of year, with you all. I love the holiday season, the collective giving of thanks—a nation focused on being grateful, even if only for a moment. I love the season of giving, of receiving, of hope. We tend to be more openhearted this time of year, more open-minded as we look around us at the people who share our world, if not our lives. We tend to be more forgiving.

It is for this reason that I bring you this particular story now. Leslie Sanderson did not have a typical childhood. Oh, she lived on the right side of the tracks, did not want for anything materially. She had a family who loved her. She had opportunity and intelligence. She got good grades and stayed away from alcohol and drugs. And she suffered unspeakably in a way that many suffer, a way of which few speak. But this Christmas, at the age of thirty-one, Leslie chooses to speak. Trusting in the promise that the season has always represented to her, she makes the choice to live life fully, instead of allowing it to hold her hostage. I love Leslie. I love everything she stands for. I love her strength, her weakness, her willingness to get up each day and try again. And I love her jewelry! So much so that I own a number of identical pieces.

The Promise of Christmas is not a fable or a fairy tale. And yet, as I read it one final time, I felt as victorious as I ever did reading those stories of triumph. In this book, Leslie and Kip and their family find the promise that is real, not fantasy—the promise that love truly is strong enough to conquer all. Even the unseen demons that live inside.

From my heart to yours, Merry Christmas!

Tara Taylor Quinn

P.S. I love to hear from readers. You can reach me at P.O. Box 133584, Mesa, Arizona 85216, or through my Web site at www.tarataylorquinn.com.

THE PROMISE
OF CHRISTMAS
Tara Taylor Quinn

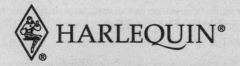

TORONTO • NEW YORK • LONDON
AMSTERDAM • PARIS • SYDNEY • HAMBURG
STOCKHOLM • ATHENS • TOKYO • MILAN • MADRID
PRAGUE • WARSAW • BUDAPEST • AUCKLAND

ISBN 0-373-71309-6

THE PROMISE OF CHRISTMAS

www.eHarlequin.com

Printed in U.S.A.

Books by Tara Taylor Quinn

HARLEQUIN SUPERROMANCE

567–YESTERDAY'S SECRETS
584–McGILLUS V. WRIGHT
600–DARE TO LOVE
624–NO CURE FOR LOVE
661–JACOB'S GIRLS
696–THE BIRTH MOTHER
729–ANOTHER MAN'S CHILD
750–SHOTGUN BABY
784–FATHER: UNKNOWN
817–THE HEART OF CHRISTMAS
836–HER SECRET, HIS CHILD
864–MY BABIES AND ME
943–BECCA'S BABY*
949–MY SISTER, MYSELF*
954–WHITE PICKET FENCES*
1027–JUST AROUND THE CORNER*
1057–THE SECRET SON
1087–THE SHERIFF OF SHELTER VALLEY*
1135–BORN IN THE VALLEY*
1171–FOR THE CHILDREN
1189–NOTHING SACRED*
1225–WHAT DADDY DOESN'T KNOW
1275–SOMEBODY'S BABY

HARLEQUIN SINGLE TITLE

SHELTERED IN HIS ARMS*

*Shelter Valley Stories

MIRA BOOKS

WHERE THE ROAD ENDS
STREET SMART
HIDDEN

For Pat Potter, who sat with me and talked about this very challenging book when she could have been at a Broadway play. I cherish your friendship. And for Paula Eykelhof, who didn't even flinch when I pitched this special story to her over Chinese dinner after a day-long road trip. I cherish you, too.

CHAPTER ONE

"LESLIE, THERE'S A Kip Webster here to see you."

The Kip Webster? As in her older brother's best friend Kip Webster?

"Did he say what he wants?"

Nancy Maple, Leslie's secretary of five years, shook her head. "Just wanted me to tell you he's here." The older woman raised her brows, her way of asking the question that might seem too personal if she actually verbalized it.

"I knew him in high school," Leslie said, keeping her explanation simple. "I haven't seen or spoken to him since my college graduation, but I heard he's a bigwig with Sporting International now."

SI was the company that Leslie hoped would seal her partnership in one of the nation's largest brokerage houses. As an investment counselor, she'd risen steadily up the ranks, due to her instincts as much as her analytical skills.

"You think he's here about the rumor that SI's going public?"

"What else could it be?" Leslie stood, resisting the

urge to take a peek in the gilded antique mirror hanging beside her desk, to flatten the flyaway auburn curls. "I'll see him," she said, shoving papers back into their file. "Send him in."

Nancy nodded. "By the way, great call on the South Seas deal. Congratulations!"

Leslie grinned, but said nothing. She'd gone against the firm's senior partners on that one, and the payoff had been bigger than even she'd expected. Several of Tyler Investments' clients were much richer today because of Leslie's recommendation that they buy into a company that could've gone under but instead went public and skyrocketed overnight.

Damn, that felt good.

Her stomach didn't feel so good right now, though. It couldn't seem to decide whether to swarm with anxiety or give in to the weight of nausea.

With her secretary gone, she took a quick glance in the mirror, decided her curls were behaving themselves today, looking not bad against the shoulders of the navy suit she'd worn to work. And her lipstick was still on.

Kip Webster. Her one and only high school crush. She wasn't ready. Juliet would disagree. Her therapist would say she could handle this. Without so much as a blip on her emotional monitor.

She reminded herself that Juliet was gifted, a miracle worker, really, as she waited for Kip's knock. Juliet wouldn't make a serious mistake like setting Leslie free if Leslie wasn't ready.

So maybe she was having a relapse, if one had such things when it came to the afflictions of one's past. Juliet had taught her how to shine a light on old shames and render them powerless, but right now she'd be happy if the ten years separating her and the darkness of her youth stretched into another fifty. Or eighty. That would put her at 110 and by then, surely, she'd be blessed with forgetfulness?

Her office door flew open and Kip was there, with the same dark hair that she'd always figured would be as curly as hers if he'd let it grow more than a quarter-inch. Same great shoulders in a tweed jacket she'd never seen before. Her overreaction to him was the same in Phoenix as it had always been in the Columbus, Ohio, suburb where they'd all grown up.

"God, Les, you look phenomenal."

Same brown eyes that she'd always feared saw too much.

And just like that, ten years of sane and peaceful living disappeared as though they'd never been.

"You don't have to sound so surprised by that," she chuckled, trying desperately to find the quiet place inside herself that Juliet had helped her discover.

"I guess I *am* surprised. You…your…" His eyes scanned the short skirt of the tailored suit to her long legs. Those legs, not to mention the rest of her body, had brought her shame and embarrassment during her adolescence—feelings made worse by a promiscuous period in college. With a lot of help, mostly

from books, she'd learned to feel pride in them—
sometimes. *Please, God, don't let there be a run in
my hose.*

"Yes?" she asked, with a small grin that on another
woman probably spoke of self-assurance and play-
fulness. On Leslie, it was a carefully learned response—all part of the game of "let's pretend" that
she'd devised when she'd reinvented herself.

"You grew up."

"We all do, eventually." She came around to the
front of her desk. As she leaned against it, her jacket
fell open to reveal just a bit of the snug red pullover she had on beneath it. She'd worn her blue-
and-red Sorrelli jewelry today and the expensive
Swarovski, Austrian crystal gave her confidence,
reminded her that she was a woman who deserved
to be happy and who wasn't afraid to go after what
she wanted.

She'd hot-flashed for days after buying her first
piece of the designer jewelry. She'd gone back twice
to return the beautiful pair of earrings, and each time
had heard Juliet's voice in the back of her head, reminding her that she was worthy.

Today, tucked away in the jewelry armoire in a
corner of her large master suite at home, was Sorrelli
jewelry in every color and style she could find.

"I'm sorry. Did you say something?" she asked.
Kip had taken a step toward her, watching her, while
she'd been busy searching for inner peace.

"I said you did it better than most." He was coming closer.

She blinked and smiled wider to prevent herself from cracking into a million little pieces.

"Grew up, I mean." He was right in front of her, his lips smiling. Close.

Aha. He was still making small talk. Meanwhile she'd started thinking about what it would be like to kiss him. How could she still be entertaining the thought, the *fantasy,* that had practically consumed her in high school?

"Yes, well…" She stood, slid away from him before he could touch her and practically jumped to a safe position behind her massive teak desk. "I've been known to get things right sometimes."

All the time really, at least professionally. But then, professionally was the only way anyone knew her.

Except Juliet, of course—although, technically, even that relationship was professional.

Juliet, where are you when I need you?

"I know this is a surprise, my showing up like this," Kip said, hands hanging down, crossed in front of him. "And I apologize for that—"

"No!" she said too quickly, eager to make up for the fact that she'd just turned away from him. "Don't be sorry. I'm…glad to see you!" How she'd been able to speak in that tone, and to keep her smile, was beyond her.

"The thing is…I'm—" He stopped, his expression

becoming almost morose as he glanced away, and Leslie's smile faded.

"I'm assuming you're here representing Sporting International." Taking the offensive gave her strength. "And I want to assure you—and your owners—that…"

Leslie's voice dried up in her throat as Kip turned back to her. "I'm not here on business, Les." She didn't recognize the low intensity in his voice. Kip had seldom been without a hint of teasing in his tone. With her, anyway.

He thrust his hands into the pockets of his slacks.

"What then?" Leslie picked up a random file from the corner of her desk. She didn't want to know. No matter what it was, she didn't want to know.

"I— There's no easy way to…"

The file said Berkeley on it. Typed in all black caps on a yellow label. Nancy color-coded everything. Yellow for potential clients, blue for—

"Cal's dead, Les." Kip took his hands from his pockets and reached out to her. His eyes, for the second she couldn't keep herself from meeting them, were moist and warm. Pulling her in. "There was—"

"No," she said with all the authority her success had earned her. "I just spoke with him two days ago. He's rock-climbing in the Rockies. I know, because he wanted to fly out here first, but I have a couple of big meetings this week, a New York turnaround, so there was no way I could…"

She repeated the usual excuse of business commitments with the regret she'd mastered over the years.

"There was an accident," Kip said, coming around her desk. She felt his fingers through the sleeves of her jacket. He couldn't touch her. She couldn't let him. Didn't he understand that?

She stood motionless, wondering about color codes. And coping.

"His foot slipped. It was trapped between two boulders. When he yanked to free himself he flew backward, somehow got tangled in his line…"

Yes? And? You don't die…of entanglement. Cal wasn't dead. He owed her something. She wasn't sure what. But he couldn't die without somehow making it up to her…

"He was already gone by the time they got to him," Kip said. "They said it was pretty much instant."

"He strangled himself?" she asked. A strange twist of justice? No! Leslie recoiled from her own thoughts. Her brother was one of the most caring men she'd ever known. For years he'd been the one she looked to for security.

"He hit his head."

Oh. That could be serious. But *dead?*

"Les?" Kip's grip on her arms tightened. He drew her closer. She didn't want him to hold her, but rested her head on his chest for just a second anyway. So she could think. "I'm so sorry, honey."

He was sorry for her. She couldn't have that. Leslie nodded, gripping the front of his shirt with both hands. "I'm sorry you had to do this." She found a way to speak. "He was your best friend. I know you've got to be in shock…."

His only reply was a single movement of the chin that rested on top of her head. And the brief sob that shook the body so close to hers. Leslie tried to stand outside herself and watch. As she searched frantically for the still, calm place that brought her peace, she felt a sympathy sob coming on. Just one. For Kip.

After that, she didn't remember much.

"DEARLY BELOVED, we are gathered here this Thanksgiving Day to mourn the passing, celebrate the life of, and be thankful for having known Calhoun Olmstead Sanderson, a young man who…"

Dressed all in black, suit, shirt, tie, shoes, Kip stood between the two Sanderson women in a small corner of the barren and brown cemetery in Westerville, Ohio, warding off the chill. That gray November day God had been considerate enough to postpone the cold spell that would consume the state of Ohio for most of the next several months. It was a balmy forty-eight degrees. It could have been below freezing for all Kip noticed.

"…At the age of twelve young Calhoun lost his lawyer father in a drive-by shooting and from that point on took up the reins of man of the house, often voluntarily forgoing his own teenaged pleasures to serve the needs of his small family—mostly, at that time, babysitting his nine-year-old sister, Leslie…"

The jolt next to him was his cue. Kip slid an arm around the slender body of his best friend's little sister. She'd broken down the night before at the viewing, and at the funeral home a couple of days before that, and when she'd walked by the room in her mother's house that had been her brother's when they'd all lived there together.

Cal had practically raised Leslie. She'd idolized him. Kip had expected her to take his death hard…

"…A scholar, a gifted football quarterback who gave up his shot at the NFL to follow in his father's footsteps in the legal profession so he could be close at hand in the event that either his mother or sister needed him…"

Leslie slumped and Kip held her against him. She was crying quietly again, not making a sound as the tears poured down her cheeks. He swallowed, his throat thick.

Kip Webster had felt a lot of things for a lot of different women in his thirty-three years. He loved everything about women—their emotions, the combination of intelligence and intuition, the softness. His idea of heaven was being the only man among a universe of happy women. Not many men could handle such a feat—keeping that many of them happy. He was pretty confident he could.

Or he had been. Until four days ago, when Calhoun Sanderson's little sister fell apart in his arms behind the very impressive desk of her very impressive office in the swankiest building in downtown Phoenix. He would help her. Handle whatever needed to be handled. He'd take care of everything. His friend would have wanted that.

Clara Sanderson's best friend, Mary something-or-other, stood to the right of the casket and started to sing. "Oh, Lord my God, when I in awesome wonder, consider all the worlds thy hands have made…"

Needing both arms to take Leslie's full weight, Kip pulled her up against him. It would all be over soon and she could get out of there. He'd carry her if he had to.

"…I see the stars, I hear the roaring thunder…"

He licked lips so dry they hurt. He couldn't believe Cal was really gone. A loyal friend, attentive son, adoring older brother, he was one of the few men Kip truly respected. He'd been the reason Kip had made it to college; he'd cajoled Kip to go with him to the University of Michigan, to get out of the Columbus life of hard living, drinking too much, doing expensive drugs, drag racing—all things his father's money had provided and his father's neglect had allowed.

Cal had moved home to Columbus after graduation. Kip had stayed in Ann Arbor, got on with SI, and the rest was history.

"…When Christ shall come with shout of acclamation to take me home…"

Leslie's head fell gently against his shoulder. Her

body felt so unbelievably good. Familiar—though, other than a teasing punch on the shoulder, he couldn't remember ever touching her before.

She felt…genuine. A safe harbor.

That seemed crazy when she couldn't even stand on her own.

The minister said a few final words, and then it was time for Leslie and her mother to take one last walk by the casket, to leave their roses on the grave.

"Les?" He pulled away, glanced down at the face streaked with makeup and tears. She stared vacantly back at him—reminding him for one scary second of someone in a state of shock.

"It's time," he said softly.

She nodded. Kip supported her as she said her final goodbyes to her only sibling and then stumbled back to the car. She didn't even seem to notice the people watching her, those judging her ability to cope, those offering love and support. She was lost someplace. On her own.

With a last glance back at the only real friend he'd ever had, Kip sent up a silent promise. He'd watch out for Leslie and Clara.

"WHO'S THAT OLD LADY, Nana?"

Ada King tightened her grip on the bony little shoulders of the five-year-old boy beside her. They stood at the back of the small crowd gathered at the Lakeview cemetery.

"That's your daddy's mama."

"She doesn't *look* mean." Jonathan's childish voice belied the wisdom in his tear-drenched eyes.

"She's not mean, child." Ada adjusted the little girl draped over her right shoulder. Kayla had fallen asleep shortly after they'd arrived. Ordinarily that would've been just fine, but at sixty-two Ada's bones weren't as able to withstand the two-year-old's weight as they might have twenty-five years ago, when she'd been raising the children's mother.

"But she won't let me be up there with Daddy."

Ada's arm dropped from Jonathan's shoulder. "Come, child," she said, turning toward the sedan Calhoun Sanderson had bought for Abby right after she'd had Jonathan. Jonathan was too smart to be just five. And Ada was tired.

Too tired. The children needed someone with a body that didn't ache every minute of every day, someone whose legs could still run and whose eyes could still see all the little things that tiny fingers reached for.

"She's white."

"Yes, child."

"Like Daddy."

"Yes, child."

"Is she mad 'cause me and Kayla ain't?"

Ada unlocked the car, transferred the sleeping girl to her car seat in the middle of the back. Kayla's frizzy little braids were glued to the side of her head with sweat.

"Aren't, child. Not ain't." She double-checked the safety latch across Kayla's chest.

Jonathan stared at her as he climbed in to the front passenger seat. "You say ain't."

"I'm old."

The skinny little black boy buckled his seat belt around the church slacks she'd laid out for him that morning and stared out the side window at his father's grave.

Ada ached for a good long cry.

"THANK YOU ALL FOR COMING," Attorney Jim Brackerfield stood at the door of the conference room in the downtown Columbus office that housed his firm. It was Friday morning. Leslie barely gave her brother's partner a glance; she was more concerned with her mother's comfort, with breathing calmly through the next few minutes. She could hardly believe only four days had passed since she'd been standing in her own office congratulating herself on a South Seas deal that now seemed far more distant than mere miles away—despite her daily calls to Nancy.

Kip pulled out chairs at the conference table for her and her mother. Smiling her thanks, Leslie smoothed the gray wool skirt beneath her and sat facing the north wall, the window of which looked out toward Ohio State University. Her alma mater.

"I would've been happy to come to the house," Jim was saying to Clara.

"I know, Jim, and that means a lot. Thanks," Clara said, her lips trembling. "But I needed to come here, to see his…the office without him in it…."

Leslie nodded, rubbed the crystals in her necklace, shades of blue and gray and black. She'd agreed with her mother's decision to meet the attorney at his office.

While her mother and Jim, who knew each other well, talked about mutual acquaintances who'd been at the funeral the day before, Kip took the seat next to her. She hadn't been surprised to hear that Cal had left something in his will for his closest friend.

His sports equipment, she'd bet.

She smiled at him a second time, glad he was there. She was doing much better today, now that the whole process of saying goodbye to Cal was behind them. Still, Kip's presence was…a blessing.

Jim sat on the other side of the long table. He was older than her brother by at least ten years, his hair thinning and gray, but judging by his athletic frame, he'd shared her brother's passion for sports.

"I…" He coughed, looked down at the papers in his hands, put on a pair of reading glasses. Took them off.

"Oh, hell." He pushed the papers away. "Cal's will is here. We can read it together or apart, whatever you prefer. But I know what it says, and there's just no easy way to tell you—"

"None of us needs my brother's money, Jim," Leslie said, relying on her years of professional experience to put the other man at ease. "Even if he's left it to…to historic car research, we'll all support his choice."

Clara patted Leslie's thigh under the table, reaching for her daughter's hand. "She's right," Clara added.

Kip nodded.

"He didn't leave his assets—and they were considerable, by the way—to historic car research."

Leslie waited, honestly unconcerned with anything but enduring this for her mother's sake and getting out of there, as soon as she could. She'd used an antique gold clip to pull her hair back, but wished she'd let it hang free to curtain her face.

"He didn't leave them to any of you, either."

"Calhoun felt the weight of responsibility for all he'd been given," Clara said softly. "He knew that neither Leslie nor I needed his money. It truly is fine, Jim. I'd just like to know who he chose to help…."

Let it be meaningful, Leslie thought. *Please let his last grand gesture be full of heart and compassion.*

Jim tapped the tips of his fingers together, glancing down again. His gaze, when it met each of theirs in turn, was grave.

"He left it to his children…."

Leslie's skin chilled. Her fingers, sliding from her mother's, were clammy.

"His…" Clara's face was white, pasty-looking beneath makeup that no longer enhanced her skin, her lips thin and pinched.

Calhoun had children. Leslie's heart raced, filled with fear, and then settled into an uneasy pace. *God, please let them be well-loved. Safe. Protected.*

She'd been all of those things.

No! Let them be…oh, she didn't know what. *Please, God, let it be okay. If something happened to them, if I could've done something…*

"I should've known," she muttered, "should never have stayed away so long."

"Your mother was right here in town and she didn't know…." Jim's voice seemed to come from far off.

"It can't be true," Clara interrupted, sounding lost. "He would've told me. Cal was a loving son. Attentive. He was over for dinner every Sunday, took me to the theater, visited during the week. He would never have kept my grandchildren from me."

Jim cleared his throat. "He—"

"He wasn't even married!" Clara blurted, rubbing one hand up and down the skirt of her violet suit and pulling at the lapel of her jacket with the other. At seventy, Clara Sanderson was retired, but in her day, she'd been every bit as formidable in the business world as her daughter was now. Where Leslie's forte was finance, Clara's had been real estate.

Leslie took her mother's hand under the table, as much to still her own jitters as to calm her mother's.

"Be that as it may, your son had two children, Mrs. Sanderson," Jim said, leaning forward as he spoke.

"And he left them everything," Kip said, as though trying to sum up what they'd been told and get them out of there. Or at least, that was what Leslie hoped he was doing.

"Not quite," Jim said, looking from Kip to Leslie. "He left the two of you something quite valuable, too."

Leslie didn't want anything of Cal's. She just wanted to get outside, breathe, figure out what to do next.

"I can't imagine what that would be," Kip said, frowning.

Cal had kids someplace and presumably Jim knew where. She had to find them. Hell, she didn't even know how old they—

"He left you the kids," the attorney's voice was like a loud crack in the silence. "To you, Kip, he left guardianship of his five-year-old son, Jonathan. And Leslie, he asked that you take two-year-old Kayla."

CHAPTER TWO

IT WAS ALL TOO incredible to believe. She was a mother. A mother! No, she wasn't. She could be a guardian. If she chose to accept Calhoun's final wishes.

Chose to accept. She couldn't turn her back on a two-year-old child!

"I realize that you live in Phoenix, Ms. Sanderson, and expect you might need to get back soon. A temporary order can be issued immediately for you to take the child with you if that's what you decide."

"Hold on." Kip stood, his slacks a lot more creased than they'd been when he sat down less than twenty minutes before. "Who are these children? Where are they? Where's their mother? Why haven't we heard about them until now? Who's taking care of them? Where do they live?"

All questions she should have asked. Would have asked if she'd been able to think.

Jim nodded, glanced at Clara and then directed his answer to Kip, who was standing by the window, gazing back at him through narrowed eyes.

"A little over seven years ago, Cal met a woman while arguing a case in court. She was the bailiff. The way he explained it to me—just after Kayla was born and he set up a trust for the kids, and changed his will—he'd never met a woman like her. Her name was Abby and he said she made him feel complete in ways he'd never felt before. His actual words, if I remember them correctly—" he glanced at Clara and Leslie before returning his attention to Kip "—was that when he was with her, he felt accepted, forgiven for the parts of himself he wasn't proud of. He didn't tell me what he meant by that, what he'd done, or believed he'd done. But he said that with Abby, he felt worthy. Those were his exact words."

"That's ridiculous," Clara said. "Cal was a wonderful human being, always giving, thinking of others. I told him all the time how much I appreciated him. I heard other people say similar things. He didn't suffer from feelings of unworthiness…."

Her mother was breathing heavily, but otherwise she appeared to be taking the news a whole lot better than Leslie was.

Jim shrugged. "I'm only telling you what he told me."

"So why wouldn't he have told any of us about her?" Kip asked, coming back to his seat at the table.

"She was…different from him…."

None of this was making sense to Leslie. "Cal wasn't a snob," she said.

"And he knew we weren't, either," Clara added. "We've always been an accepting bunch."

"Different, how?" Kip asked from over by the window.

"Abby was African-American." The shock of Jim's words shot through Leslie, not because she cared about Abby's race, but because her brother had always been so careful to behave conventionally. "The kids are biracial."

"So?" Clara didn't even blink. "They're my grandchildren."

She turned to Leslie then, grinning, tears in her eyes, her face pale. "I'm a grandma," she said.

"Yes, you are," Leslie told her, finding a smile for the woman she adored. Clara might not have protected Leslie in all the ways Leslie would've liked, but she'd been the best mother she could be. Leslie had never doubted that she was loved. Cared for. Supported.

"YOU SAID *WAS*." Kip hadn't yet found anything to smile about in the news they'd just been given. He needed facts.

And a night with a good woman. He didn't need a five-year-old child. Didn't know the first thing about raising children. Could hardly remember having been one himself.

Jim's raised brow was his only response.

"You said this Abby woman *was* African-American. I'm assuming she didn't have a racial transplant."

He could feel both Sanderson women looking at him, but couldn't meet their eyes. He could take care of them. But he couldn't raise a little boy.

"Abby died shortly after Kayla was born." Jim's expression softened, his words low. "A gravel truck ran a red light. She died instantly."

"So who's watching the children?" Clara seemed to be handling the situation far better than he was. Leslie was completely still.

"A woman named Ada King. She was a friend of Abby's mother, took Abby in when the mother died of cancer. Abby was only three. She'd been living with Abby since just before Jonathan was born. They owned a condominium in Westerville."

It was a nice suburb, north of Columbus. Upper middle class.

"Did Cal live there, too?" Leslie sounded as though she couldn't imagine her brother deserting his own kids.

Kip agreed with her. Cal cared. Maybe too much.

Jim shook his head. "From the little he told me, Abby wouldn't agree to marry him, and wouldn't let him live there. She'd had a hard life, needed her independence—and wasn't willing to face society's reactions to their union. She also said she wasn't going to make her children's lives harder by exposing them to the curious glances inherent in having parents from two different races. But I gather Calhoun spent a lot of time with them anyway. She and the kids were frequent visitors to his home in Gahanna as well."

The room was warm, comfortable. The light blues in the upholstery and picture frames an easy contrast with the off-white walls. It was a room designed to put people at ease. To Kip it felt like prison. He sat back down.

"How old is Ada King?"

"Sixty-two."

Still young enough to care for children. Kip nodded.

Clara leaned forward, both arms on the table in front of her. "Have you met her?"

Jim nodded. "She was at the funeral yesterday."

Kip hadn't seen a black woman there. "And the children?" Clara asked.

"They were there, too. In the back. Jonathan cried some. Kayla was asleep."

"Oh, my God." Leslie jolted beside him, and Kip wished he knew what she was thinking. Wondered if she felt anywhere near as trapped and inadequate as he did by the unexpected "gift" they'd both received.

"The poor little guy," Leslie said. "First losing his mother, then his father…"

Kip's entire body stiffened as unexpected, intense emotion grabbed hold of him. He'd just had a flash-back, knew something about being a young boy, after all. He knew exactly how it felt, how utterly terrified he'd been when, a few days after his sixth birthday, they'd buried his mother.

"When can we see them?" Leslie and Clara asked almost simultaneously.

"Anytime you'd like, but there's more that you should know first," Jim said, his glasses back on his nose as he picked up some papers. "Calhoun left a generous sum of money for Ada, and with the rest he set up a trust for the kids." He peered at Kip over the top of the wire frames. "Kip, you and Leslie are both named as trustees."

The rope around Kip's neck tightened, as he became responsible for more duties he hadn't asked for and didn't want.

Leslie glanced at him, her lips turned up in a tentative smile that failed to hide the panic in her eyes. Seeing her discomfort had an odd effect on him; it quieted his own sense of impending doom. He wasn't alone here. Together he and Leslie would figure a way out.

"You said a temporary order could be issued immediately," she said, her gaze back on the attorney. "Does that mean we could have immediate access to the kids?"

"It does."

"What about Ada King?" The returning strength in Clara's voice was a relief. "Does she know about us? About the will? Will she be resistant to our visit?"

Jim's face broke into a grin for the first time since they'd entered the room. "Ada's known about you all since the first time Abby brought Calhoun home. She knows about the will. Cal discussed it with her before he ever came to see me. After Abby died, Ada was willing to continue caring for the children as long as Calhoun was around to help. But I think that though she's going to miss those children terribly, she's relieved to know she won't be raising them all by herself. I spoke with her the day after Cal's accident. Kayla's an active little thing and Ada's getting old, can't keep up. And she has a sister in Florida who's invited Ada to share her retirement condo...."

Kip loosened the top button on the shirt that was sticking to his perspiring skin. Life just didn't damn well work this way. A man didn't get up in the morning, and find himself a parent three hours later. Raising children required knowledge he didn't have. A man didn't just take an orphan boy home with him and suddenly become equipped to father him.

"Can we have some time to think about this?" Leslie's question brought a surge of cool relief. "Until tomorrow?"

"Of course." Jim stood. "I have copies of the will for each of you. For obvious reasons Cal wanted its contents to remain undisclosed until now. Read it over and give me a call when you're ready."

Kip accepted his packet and escorted the women out into the cold Ohio day, Jim's parting words ringing in his mind. Call when he was ready? He'd *never* be ready.

JONATHAN STOOD in the doorway of the upstairs bathroom, watching as Nana braided Kayla's hair. Her fingers moved real fast over and under and on top and around, and the hair just went into place. He wasn't ever going to be able to do that. 'Specially not with his little sister squirming the whole time.

"What's gonna happen to us?" He kinda felt like throwing up as he waited for Nana's answer. But he had to find out, didn't he? If he was the only man now…

"I don't know, child."

He could see himself in the mirror. His face, which was just a boy face, was there. And his hair was boy hair, too, and Nana cut it a lot, so the red color that was like Daddy's didn't really show. His skin was always the same though he prayed till he fell asleep that he'd wake up with light skin like Kayla's, instead of dark like Nana's and Mama's. The older kids at school weren't going to call her zebra and skunk and white chocolate and swiss roll and salt and pepper and a bunch of other things he didn't know what they meant.

"It's because I'm black, isn't it?"

"What's that, boy?"

"Why they don't wanna know me and Kayla? Because I'm black and they don't want no half 'n half."

Jonathan jumped back from the door when Nana dropped her comb and whirled at him. "Don't you *never* say nothin' like that again, boy, you hear me? Not *ever*."

Jonathan nodded. And stayed real quiet. He knew better than to talk back to Nana when her face got all pointy like that.

But just 'cause he didn't say nothin' didn't mean he wasn't thinkin' it. So…he'd wait some, but if he got too scared about his baby sister and stuff, he'd just shove as much as he could carry in his special back-pack that Daddy and him went to get for school, and go far away, so they wouldn't be thinkin' bad thoughts about Kayla 'cause of him. Kayla's skin looked almost the same as Daddy's. They'd like her fine.

He'd bet that old crying lady that Nana said was Daddy's mama could make her fingers do Kayla's braids. 'Course she was old, but pro'bly she had a sister like Nana's who wanted to take care of her and would take care of Kayla, too.

"CAN I GET YOU SOMETHING to drink?" Leslie stood behind the wet bar in her mother's family room Friday evening. Clara was at a friend's house for an impromptu gathering of the six or seven women who'd raised their children together and supported each other through all the following phases of their lives. Which left her and Kip alone—both guests in her mother's house.

"Bourbon would be great." Kip flipped on the switch for the gas fire, leaning an arm on the hand-carved mahogany mantel as he stared toward the flames. He'd said very little since leaving the attorney's office that morning.

Not that she'd been all that communicative, either.

She'd spent most of the afternoon listening to Clara. Helped deal with the myriad details of closing down a life. And spent a couple of hours on the phone with Nancy, checking on details at work.

"Rocks or no?"

He didn't glance up from the fire.

"Rocks, please."

After getting his drink, she poured herself a glass of Riesling. Her mother had redecorated this room since Leslie had lived at home. It didn't look anything like Leslie remembered. And still, she was uncomfortable here.

Shrugging off things that had no rightful place in her life, or mind, she handed Kip his drink, losing herself for the briefest of seconds in his compassionate brown gaze.

Until she had to look away. She curled up on the end of the plush rose-colored sofa closest to the fire, instead. She hadn't been warm since she'd arrived in Ohio.

"I keep thinking about those kids in foster care…." Kip's voice trailed off as he once again stared into the gas flames that bounced almost rhythmically, creating the same splashes of amber and gold color over and over again.

"Foster care?" She hadn't meant to come across so defensively, but his comment took her completely off guard.

He turned holding the bourbon he'd asked for but

not yet touched. "Isn't that where orphan children go these days? Into foster care?"

The chill that had been surrounding her for days intensified, leaving her adrift, alone in an Alaska-like wilderness.

"You don't intend to honor Cal's wishes." All day long, in the confusing array of possibilities that had tortured her mind, she'd never once considered that they wouldn't somehow provide for Cal's children.

He sat on the edge of a maroon-flowered armchair, his feet on the intricately designed wool rug that covered most of the beige-carpeted floor, his bourbon glass held with both hands between his knees. "Do you?" He sounded as surprised as she felt.

Leslie took a sip of wine. Set the glass on the table. Clasped her hands together, shoulders hunched, and shivered. "I honestly don't know what I think," she told him, meeting his eyes. "The problems are so vast I can hardly even begin to make a list of them. I live in Phoenix. You live here. The kids would be separated. If I took Kayla, my mother would only get to see her once or twice a year. Aside from the fact that I'd lose a job I love and my means of support as well, I absolutely *cannot* move back to Ohio. My home—hell, my life—is not equipped to handle a toddler. The smell of vomit makes me vomit. I know plenty about the world of finance and nothing at all about potty-training. I work long hours, travel. I've been known to swear on occasion…."

Hearing herself, Leslie flushed.

Kip was grinning at her. "I don't think that last one disqualifies you from much of anything—including sainthood."

In spite of herself, her state of mind and inner turmoil, she smiled back. She'd always loved the times Kip was in their home.

"My brother knew me well," she said. "He knew there'd be no way in hell I could turn my back on a two-year-old orphaned child, let alone one of my own flesh and blood. Add to that my only brother's dying wish that I care for his beloved daughter." She took another sip of wine. "If I desert that child, I'll lie in bed every night hearing her cry and feeling Calhoun turning over in his grave."

"You're one intense woman, you know that?" Kip asked, taking a sip of bourbon. "And you have a way with words, too."

"So, am I wrong?"

He shrugged. "How would I know how you react to vomit?"

Leslie swirled the wine left in her glass. She had a one-glass-a-night rule, but tonight she'd already given herself permission to break it.

"The thing is, I'm also fully aware that any decisions I make affect you, too."

"How so?"

She watched him for a moment, trying to remain impartial to the way his short dark hair tried to curl around his head, to the broad shoulders and the muscled thighs in the tight jeans he'd changed into when they got back here that morning.

Leslie was still wearing the gray wool suit she'd had on. She was comfortable in the persona her work clothes gave her.

"You going to tell me it wouldn't give you a few bad nights if I decide to take Kayla and you turn Jonathan over to the state?" she asked. "I know you, Kip Webster. There's no way you wouldn't be thinking of that little boy, not only orphaned and abandoned, but separated from his little sister, too."

His reply was to finish the rest of his bourbon in one long swallow. Before she could offer him another, he was walking over to the bar.

"And if you do take him and I take Kayla to Phoenix, we'd eventually feel compelled to provide opportunities for them to see each other. We'd have to decide how to handle communication and visits and maybe even have to spend some time together at Christmas. Or at least arrange to let the kids do so."

She had no idea where any of this was coming from—she supposed from that subconscious part of her mind Juliet was always telling her about. It was leading her to other difficult conclusions, too.

Like the possibility of taking Jonathan as well as Kayla if Kip really didn't want him. Realistically, how could she even consider that?

When Kip came back with a full glass, he settled on the other end of the couch.

"And there's another whole issue we haven't even touched on," she said slowly, frowning. "It affects our decision, either way."

"What's that?"

"These kids are of mixed race. That can create psychological problems if they're not given the right kind of emotional support."

"I guess so, but how do you know that?"

Leslie smiled fleetingly. "I spend a lot of time on planes. Reading magazines because I can't concentrate on business when half my energy's consumed with keeping the plane in the air."

"You didn't read on the way here."

She could hardly remember the trip. She owed him for her ticket, she was sure, as she didn't remember buying it, either.

"I took a sleeping pill."

He sat forward, elbows on his knees as he stared into the fire again. "So tell me what you think about this whole mixed-race thing."

Leslie leaned an arm against the side of the couch, tucking her feet underneath her. "I haven't thought about it all that much," she told him honestly. "Except that I know there'll be issues. I realize you're seeing more mixed-race marriages these days, but there are still a lot of small-minded people and raised eyebrows.

"The little I know about black culture is fairly stereotypical and probably not very accurate. African-Americans have their own concerns that we can understand intellectually but not emotionally. These kids face the risk of not being accepted by either group—whites or blacks."

Kip glanced sideways at her, nodded. "And if we take Kayla and Jonathan, we'll be facing that risk with them."

"I wouldn't even know how to comb Kayla's hair!"

"I wonder if Abby celebrated Kwanza with them."

"People might stare. The bigoted ones might show disapproval." She couldn't even begin to contemplate the struggles Jonathan and Kayla could encounter in their lives. "And I wonder if being of mixed race could lessen their chances of being adopted. Especially Jonathan, since he's older. At the very least, it could reduce the available choices, since they'd only be able to pass as the biological children of a mixed-race couple. A lot of people don't want it automatically known that their kids are adopted. They want it to look as though the kids could be theirs biologically."

Kip sat back, taking a smaller sip from his glass. "I hadn't thought of that," he said. "And to take it a step further, they *could* be more at risk for abuse in a foster home, if that was where they ended up. You hear about the abuse that goes on in some of them, and I'd guess that a kid who didn't look like the rest of the kids would be more of a target. As much as we like to think differently, even in the twenty-first century there's still far too much prejudice among us."

Leslie was moved by his clearsightedness and his compassion. Moved by it and persuaded. Her decision was made. Saturday or not, she was calling Jim in the morning. She wanted those temporary orders issued—for both kids—and permanent ones started, as well.

Whatever it took, she was going to find a way to make this work.

CHAPTER THREE

"YOU'VE BEEN UP ALL NIGHT?"

Shirt unbuttoned, shoes on the floor, Kip lay back on the couch in Clara's family room and watched as Leslie, dressed in a black running suit and tennis shoes, came in. He'd heard her on the stairs.

"I dozed off," he told her, stretching the truth a bit. He'd been in a kind of trance, but wasn't sure he'd ever really slept as the dark hours dragged by. "Being here in this house, trying to make sense of the present, to figure out the future, I found myself wandering back to the past. Did you know that Cal once told me he was never going to have kids?"

Leslie perched on the arm of the chair across from him. "Don't most guys think that way in high school?"

"I sure did." Lethargic, Kip didn't move, just lay there with his arms at his sides, head propped up on the arm of the couch. If he didn't get up, he wouldn't have to face the first decision in his life that just might be too big for him. "I didn't change my mind about it, either."

"You don't have to take him, Kip," Leslie said, her blue eyes soft. She'd pulled her mass of auburn curls into a ponytail on top of her head. Even without makeup she was beautiful.

God, how she'd grown up. He'd thought about that during the long night, too. Vacillated between great interest in the new Leslie, and anger at her for changing from the kid sister she'd always been. Angry at her for tempting him.

"I was thinking about the time Cal and I came out of the locker room after a particularly great Friday-night game to find the Saylor twins waiting. They'd set aside the whole night just for us. I thought I'd died and gone to heaven."

Kip grinned at Leslie as he relived, just for a second, those easier days of youth when things had seemed black and white rather than the confusing shades of gray he now knew them to be.

"From what I remember, that was all in a day's work for the two of you," Leslie said, smiling back. "Or a night's…"

"Yeah, well, the Saylor twins were…special."

"Loose you mean."

"Generous is how I'd describe them."

Shaking her head, Leslie grinned even more. "You're an embarrassment to faithful men everywhere, Kip Webster."

He should probably sit up. But it felt so damn good lying there, talking to her. Natural.

"Hey, now," he said, "I'm not unfaithful. Being unfaithful means there had to be faith to begin with. Promises and vows—which I haven't made. I've never once pretended to be anything other than what I am."

"And that is?"

He opened his mouth with a ready quip, met her eyes, and closed it again, smile fading.

"I'm honest, Les. I never allow a woman to think she's the only one in my life."

Her grin was gone, too. "Has there ever been a time there's been only one?" The question was almost a whisper.

"There've been more times when there've been none."

"No!" She reached across and yanked at his toe before dropping into the chair. "The great Kip Webster without a woman?"

"I didn't say it happened—*just* that there've been more times when I didn't have a woman than when I had only one." He didn't join her attempt to return them to the lighthearted conversation of moments ago. "You know something?" he said, completely serious. "That night when the Saylor twins were waiting for us, Cal and I had already agreed to go right home and get a good night's rest. We'd told your mother that first thing Saturday morning we'd move an elderly client of hers out of the house she'd just closed on…."

Kip could remember that night like it had been the week before.

"I was halfway to the car with the twins, fully prepared to pull an all-nighter and then help your mom, but Cal would have none of it. He said we could see the twins the next night. I thought he'd lost his mind." Kip couldn't find the smile that should have accompanied the boyhood memory. All he could find was the panic that had set in when Jim Brackerfield pronounced him guardian of a five-year-old boy.

"So you went out with the twins and Cal came home?" Leslie asked.

"No, I was spending the night at your house. And Cal was right. They agreed to see us the next night."

Swinging his legs to the floor, Kip sat up. "But that's the thing, Les. I would've gone. It never even occurred to me not to go. I'm just not the responsible type."

When she leaned forward, Kip could see a hint of the cleavage he'd first noticed when she was about fifteen and he'd been leaving for college. He'd only ever seen her twice since then, until now. At her high school and college graduations.

"You were seventeen, Kip!"

"I like women, Les. I can imagine meeting someone at a business lunch, stretching lunch to dinner and completely forgetting to pick up the kid from daycare or wherever he might be."

"Have you ever had a cat?" Leslie asked.

"Yeah, how'd you know?"

"That time mine was hit by a car and almost died

and you drove me to the vet. While we were waiting, you told me your dad wouldn't allow you to have a pet but when you were on your own you were going to get a cat. Couldn't be a dog because they had to be taken for walks and you weren't planning to be home every night."

Since her words only added weight to the dread already consuming him, Kip didn't share her humor. "See what I mean? Even then I knew I couldn't be relied on."

"Did you ever forget to feed your cat?"

"Of course not." He wasn't a complete imbecile. "He always had a clean litter box, too. He was almost ten when he got leukemia. I can't tell you the nights I sat up with him before he finally had to be put down."

"There you go," Leslie said, standing up. "You like to play, Kip, but you've never been one to shirk your responsibilities. Take that night with the Saylor twins," she said, her mischievous grin affecting him in mysterious ways, "you'd have gone, but you also would've shown up to help my mother, worked your ass off, then gone home and crashed as soon as you were done."

Maybe. But…

"And that would've been a horrible example to set," he told her. "You know me, Les. I was born wild. If it hadn't been for your family taking pity on me, I wouldn't have any idea at all of what family life's supposed to be like. And I didn't totally get it even when I *was* here. How many times did I worry your mother sick because I forgot to call when I was coming here and I was late? Or forgot to come over, period? I was arrested at sixteen for possession of an illegal substance…"

"It was a first offense, the only offense, the record was sealed when you turned eighteen and no one will ever know about it."

"I'm not prepared to be a father, Les."

"I know."

"I haven't got a clue about raising a kid."

"I know. Me, neither."

"But you're going to take her, aren't you?"

His breathing stopped during the second she nodded her head.

IN A LITTLE OVER AN HOUR, she was going to meet Cal's children. Leslie didn't have any idea how one prepared for such a thing. Should she just be herself? Wear a pantsuit and fancy jewelry and pretend she wasn't afraid, at least in some measure, almost every minute of every day?

Or should she put on the one pair of jeans she still owned—left behind from a visit to her mother six or seven years ago, when Cal had been white-water rafting—and top it with the pink sweater she'd brought to wear under her black suit? Her black boots would be fine with jeans. And she could wear the butterfly necklace from her Purple Rain collection—it had blues and pinks and violets. Little girls liked butterflies.

Oh, God, how do you expect me to do this? In bra and panties, Leslie sank onto the white eyelet coverlet on the double bed she'd slept in as a child growing up in her mother's house. She'd handled incredible pressures during her thirty years on earth, but somehow none of them seemed as insurmountable as the decision before her now. Her eye caught the rose-colored angel night-light she'd had since she was a child.

It had burned the night before. Just as a similar one burned in her own home every night. *Angel, where's your calm?*

A call to Jim Brackerfield just after breakfast that morning had resulted in this Saturday-afternoon visit with the children. Her mother was coming, too. If all went well, Leslie could take Kayla home with her to Phoenix the next day.

Staring at the white eyelet curtains, the yellow walls with their pictures of butterflies and tacked-up posters of "feel-good" quotes from her teen years, she wondered who'd be supplying the definition of "well." If it was her, there wouldn't be one.

KIP, FRESHLY SHOWERED, shaved and dressed in jeans, a beige sweater and an open brown leather jacket, was standing outside by the rental car when Leslie and her mother left the house.

"You're coming?" she asked, afraid to hope. She was determined not to sway Kip, make him feel guilty or give any indication of how much she wished he'd take her nephew—to love him. Even more than that, she wanted him to do whatever he needed to do.

"I didn't put you down as a driver on the car," he said, referring to the rental they'd brought from the airport."

"We can take mine," Clara said.

Kip opened the front passenger door for the older woman, who slid in without another word.

Leslie climbed in back, thanking God for giving her the strength Kip's presence offered—even it was only for the afternoon.

ADA KING'S WRINKLED FACE and arthritic fingers looked more like those of an eighty-year-old woman than the sixty-two they'd been told she was. Her smile was gracious and genuine when she opened the door of the three-story condominium.

"The children are downstairs in the playroom," she said. "I thought it best for you to meet them down there…." She stepped aside as they entered. "Then, if you all have any questions…"

She had a million of them. And couldn't think of one. "I'm Leslie," she said, holding out her hand.

"The picture your brother had was old, but I recognize you," Ada said, gripping her hand. "Your brother thought the sun rose and set on them curls of yours."

Leslie blinked back the tears she'd been fighting all the way across town. *Oh, Cal. How can I possibly miss you so much? How can you still matter to me? How am I ever going to love your children and not lose myself?*

After shaking hands with Clara and Kip, Ada led them toward a staircase at the back of the living room they'd entered.

"Kayla's toys are all down here," she said. "It's best to keep plenty of things handy for that one to do."

Leslie's heart started to pound. "She's active?"

"She's two," Ada said as if that explained everything, glancing over her shoulder at Leslie as they slowly descended the stairs. Kip and Clara were right behind her.

Breathe. Leslie took a step. And then another. *Real breaths, not those shallow gasps that barely keep you alive.* She heard Juliet's voice in her head.

The carpet was short, variegated browns and beiges, and thickly padded. Expensive. But easy to clean and it hid stains. There wasn't a single fingerprint on the light beige walls. She could hear a childish lisp in a high little voice, couldn't understand the words. If there'd been a reply, it had been uttered too softly to hear.

Leslie turned, met her mother's tremulous gaze, and then her eyes locked with Kip's. For a second she saw naked fear—an emotion that echoed all the way through her.

She hadn't even known these children existed until the day before. And now one of them was supposed to be hers?

And Cal's. Always Cal's. Could she raise her brother's daughter?

Could she not?

"Jonathan, Kayla, they're here to meet you," Ada said, rounding the corner at the bottom of the stairs.

Light-headed with tension—and probably lack of oxygen—Leslie turned the corner, vaguely aware of her mother and Kip coming up beside her. All she really noticed were the eyes staring at her from a mahogany-brown face topped with straight red hair, exactly the same as her brother's. Jonathan Sanderson was the most striking little boy she'd ever seen.

And then the slightest movement drew her eyes downward to the chubby little girl hugging her brother's leg. Kayla's head was covered in frizzy braids. Her overalls were pink, swarming with butterflies, as was the long-sleeved shirt she had on underneath them. And her skin was creamy beige, beautiful. Kayla was beautiful.

"Da da da?" Tears flooded Leslie's eyes the second she heard the voice. And just like that, she fell in love.

Jonathan pulled the child even closer, wrapping an arm protectively around her shoulders.

"He's not comin' back, Kayla," the little boy whispered, leaning down to his sister, but still watching the three outsiders who'd just invaded his territory. "'Member? We talked all 'bout it."

"Da da da," Kayla said again, her voice softer as she, too, stared at the strangers.

"Come forward, boy," Ada said, her hand beckoning.

So slowly he was hardly moving, Jonathan came forward, bringing his sister with him. Ada waited patiently. And when he arrived, put an arm around his skinny little shoulders.

"Jonathan Sanderson, this is your grandma." She stopped him in front of Clara, who knelt, tears streaming down her face.

"Hello, Jonathan, I'm so happy to meet you," she said quietly.

"Nice to meet you, ma'am." Jonathan peered at Clara for a moment and then back at Ada, who moved him along.

"And this is your aunt Leslie."

Leslie didn't know where the ear-to-ear grin came from, but when that little body stopped in front of her, gazing up at her with distrusting eyes, she saw a world of happy times ahead of them.

"Hi, Jonathan. I didn't even know about you until yesterday, but I'm *so* glad to meet you," she said, reaching out to touch his hair. "It's like mine."

"It's like my daddy's." The boy's chin trembled, but otherwise he was completely composed. Although Leslie had only limited familiarity with kids, that seemed unusual to her.

She knelt down beside her mother, who was still on her knees watching the children she obviously longed to pull into her arms. "You must be Kayla," she said to the little girl peering out from behind her brother.

Kayla stepped out then. Nodded. Poked her finger at Leslie's hair. "Da da da."

"She don't know what she's sayin'," Jonathan quickly inserted. He looked up at Kip, eyes narrowed. "Who's he?"

"This is Kip Webster, child," Ada said, and Leslie thought of the most important question she should've asked Ada King before they'd come downstairs. Did Jonathan know the terms of his father's will?

"Who's he?" Jonathan asked again, pretty much confirming what Leslie had feared. The little boy hadn't been told that he was about to be taken from the only home he'd ever known.

But at least if Kip decided not to take him, Jonathan wouldn't realize that Kip hadn't wanted him.

"He was your daddy's best friend from the time they were wee like you," Ada said. She dropped her arm from around the boy and stepped back.

But not too far back, Leslie noted.

The boy studied Kip for a long moment. "You want to see my radio control helicopter that really flies?" Jonathan finally asked Kip. "It's pretty cool."

Leslie watched, holding her breath.

"Sure," Kip said, smiling at the little boy with a natural ease that confirmed something Leslie had always assumed but that Kip Webster hadn't yet figured out. Someday he was going to make a wonderful father. "You got one control or two?"

THREE HOURS LATER Ada walked them to the door, but Kip wasn't ready to leave. He wasn't ready to end this segment of his life—to move on to whatever was coming next.

"We'll call you in the morning," he told the older woman in a low voice. Jonathan and Kayla were downstairs, glued to a Disney video on the large-screen TV that took up one end of the huge sitting room. Still he wouldn't put it past the precocious little guy he'd spent the past couple of hours playing with to have crept up the stairs far enough to listen in.

"Mr. Brackerfield says you might be takin' Kayla tomorrow." Ada looked at Leslie.

"I—"

"This all happened so fast," Kip interrupted and he wasn't even sure why. Driven by some unidentifiable tension inside him, he continued anyway. "You've known about these kids all their lives," he said. "We're not only grieving Cal's unexpected death, but dealing with the shock of finding out that he kept something like this from his entire family."

That wasn't it at all. But Ada was nodding so maybe she'd accept his rambling explanation as a reason for delaying any final decision.

"Just give us the evening to talk, and then we'll call you with some solid plans."

"Take all the time you need," Ada said, her expression gentle. "I ain't in no hurry. Just want to have the little one's things packed if she's got to go."

"We'll let you know," Kip said again, before Leslie could make some definite commitment.

"What was that about?" she asked him as soon as the front door of the condo closed behind them.

"I just—"

"I'm taking her, Kip." She walked to the parking lot, holding the edges of her black suede coat together as she shivered in the cold. "You aren't going to change my mind about that."

"I have no intention of trying," he admitted honestly. But that was all he could tell her. It was all he knew.

CHAPTER FOUR

CLARA SUGGESTED that Leslie and Kip go out alone for the evening, someplace neutral, and have their talk. Which was why, just after seven, Leslie found herself walking along High Street, the main drag, which ran through Ohio State University in downtown Columbus, with her high school crush beside her. Dressed in her lone pair of jeans and the pink sweater beneath her mother's borrowed winter parka, Leslie was at least glad to be out of the house.

"It's just like your mom to insist that we get away from her and all the memories of Cal at the house as we try to figure out what to do," Kip said, his breath visible in the cold night air as they walked past noisy bars interspersed with tattoo shops, fast food restaurants and closed bookstores. "She was always one to respect personal space, always trying not to pressure you unduly to her way of thinking."

"Yeah," was the only response Leslie could manage. If her mother hadn't been so determined to give her and Cal their "space," would things have turned out differently?

A group of college-age girls passed, parkas open to reveal the belly rings and bare skin that showed between the button on their jeans and the hem of their shirts. One of them knocked the shoulder strap of Leslie's black Brighton bag off her shoulder. At least three of them had been talking at once, and she wondered how any of them ever got heard.

"You hungry?" Kip asked.

"A little." They hadn't eaten since a quick sandwich before going to meet the kids. Leslie hadn't finished hers. "Not really."

Too much on her mind. "That place looks exactly like it did when I worked there." They were passing the popular hamburger joint that had provided her spending money during her undergraduate years.

"You had money from your father," Kip said, hands in the pockets of his leather jacket. "I never could understand why you'd choose to work in a fast food place."

Leslie shrugged, not expecting him to understand. "I wanted to be like everyone else." And to have long hours with lots of lights and activity and noise—to keep her from panicking her way right out of college.

Secrets isolated people, casting them into an internal darkness, a loneliness that often resulted in bouts of anxiety.

A convertible drove by with the top down and a group of husky young men wearing blue and gold University of Michigan letterman jackets sitting up on the back seat. They were whooping and hollering loudly enough to be heard at Ada King's home in Westerville fifteen miles away.

"I forgot, today was the Michigan game," Kip said. "They must've won!"

Michigan versus Ohio State was the big football rivalry, often determining which of the two teams would be playing in the biggest college bowl game at the end of the year.

"Good for them!" she said, smiling. "They won only once when I was a student here, but I wore my Michigan jersey up and down High Street that night, doing my father proud." She hadn't had many typical college weekend nights during her time at the university; that November Saturday of her junior year had been one of the few.

"I never understood why, considering the fact that both your father and grandfather graduated from U of M—and you were so obviously a fan, even when you were a kid—you chose to go to OSU."

Because Cal had been at U of M doing graduate work. "I got a full scholarship to Ohio State."

Her mom had accepted the explanation, and there was no reason to expect that Kip wouldn't.

The street was so brightly lit it could almost have been daytime, and teeming with young people intent on a night of living it up. Leslie wondered how many of them would be living it down the next morning. She'd occasionally done that, too. Never again.

"You want a drink?" Kip asked.

They needed to talk. A noisy High Street bar wasn't conducive to serious conversation. Or any conversation that could actually be heard. "Sure."

She could use a glass of wine. Take the edge off, at least a little. She was going to take Kayla. Telling Kip wouldn't be easy.

Neither was making the request she had to make—if he wasn't taking Jonathan, she wanted Kip to sign him over to her.

But then, she'd never found life particularly easy. And that hadn't stopped her yet.

LEAVE IT TO KIP to find a quiet corner in a quiet bar— one that actually served food as well as drinks—a couple of blocks down from Ohio State. There was only one other patron in the room and the hostess sat them in a scarred wooden booth all the way at the back, far from the door.

"How'd you know about this place?" she asked, the menu open in front of her.

"I didn't," he said, laying his menu down. "I'll have the steak sandwich," he told the young man who approached the table, pad in hand. "And a beer. Tall."

He'd lucked into a quiet bar on High Street. Was there nothing in Kip Webster's life that wasn't charmed? Other than his childhood, she reminded herself. From all accounts, that had been sheer hell.

Which could explain why the man felt compelled to turn his back on fatherhood.

She ordered the turkey wrap and a glass of wine. She wasn't like Kip. She *couldn't* be like him, couldn't let herself think about not doing as Cal wished. The irony of that wasn't lost on her, either.

"So what did you think?"

"About the sandwich? Quite good, thank you." She smiled across at her dinner companion, finding a curious humor in the fact that her dreams had finally come true—she was out on High Street, alone with Kip, on a Saturday night—albeit ten years too late and not quite for the reason she'd hoped. But then fate had a way of doing that to her.

"I wasn't talking about the sandwich," Kip said with a small grin. The flip-flop in her stomach had nothing to do with the food, either. And everything to do with the man.

"I'd like another glass of wine first."

"I thought they were adorable," Leslie said before her second glass of wine arrived. "I'm guessing they were on their best behavior, but they seem like really good kids."

"Jonathan's a brainiac."

"A what?"

"Brainiac," Kip said, worrying the edge of his drink napkin between his thumb and index finger.

He'd removed his jacket, and the green sweater he was wearing brought out glints of gold in his eyes. "His word, not mine. He said the kids at school call him that. Means he's smart."

Her wine was served. Leslie took a gulp, hoping she'd camouflaged the gesture as a ladylike sip. "For a five-year-old, he's far too aware of others," she said.

"You've known many five-year-olds?"

Leslie watched him for a long minute, a silent debate playing itself out as she decided how much of herself to let him know.

"I want children," Leslie said. "Not like this, not now, but I've known for quite a while that my career isn't enough to fill my life forever. I want to be a mother, to be pregnant and nurse and potty-train and…and protect."

The last word resonated through her system. Or maybe it was just the wine.

"Is there a man who's part of all this?" It was the first he'd asked about her love life, but she supposed it wasn't surprising that the topic would come up, considering they were there to discuss becoming parents—or not.

"Well." She cocked her head, hoping she could pull off the sassy smile she'd conjured up inside. "That would be why it's still just in the planning stages," she told him. "But…" She held up a hand, glad it wasn't shaking. "I am a huge believer in stating your intent and focusing on what you desire, so I visit the day care in my office building as often as I can. There are some five-year-olds there during the after-school hours."

"So you *do* have some experience."

She couldn't tell if his tone was accusatory, relieved or neutral. "I haven't actually talked to them," she said. "I just stop in, look around, make sure there aren't any kids being neglected...."

His eyes narrowed. "You're making sure that your employees' benefits are everything they should be."

He gave her that look. She'd actually forgotten it—that way he had of looking at her with his eyes warm and hinting at a deeper knowledge, as though he could see right inside her. She'd hated it at thirteen, afraid of what he might see. "Okay," she said, before he looked any deeper. "Yes, I do regular checks—informal checks—on the quality of our day care because I care about our employees. And their children."

His head tilted just a bit as he peered at her. "There's no reason to be embarrassed about that, Les," he said, no hint of laughter in his eyes, or his voice. "In fact, I respect the hell out of you for it."

She didn't have anything to say to that. So she took another sip of wine. This might end up being a three-glass night.

"You're still planning to accept guardianship of Kayla."

"Yes."

"How can you do that?" In that moment, he reminded her of himself as a twelve-year-old boy watching her mother make pancakes. He'd insisted on trying for himself and sent batter flying across the stove when he attempted to flip one.

She frowned. Whether it was due to exhaustion, wine, or just because she was with Kip Webster, Leslie felt unable to keep up the running game of *let's pretend* with which she faced her days. "You want the completely honest version?"

"Aren't you always honest?"

"To a point."

"Then yes," he said, leaning forward, arms on the table, as he held her gaze. "I want the *completely* honest version."

"I have no idea."

He sat back, still watching her. She suspected it hadn't been the answer he'd been hoping for.

"I really don't know, Kip." She glanced over as two older couples came through the door, wearing Michigan colors. Their alma mater? Were they local or had they driven in?

Had Cal taught Jonathan the "Go Blue" theme song, as their father had taught them? Would she teach Kayla?

"I just know I have to do this."

He nodded, dropped his eyes, tore slowly at his napkin. "You're really going to take her tomorrow?"

"I'd love to find a reason to delay, but I can't. I have to get back to Phoenix. I've already been away too long. And…" She waited for him to look up at her. "It might seem strange, but now that I know I'm going to be her mother, I don't want to leave without her."

"What about Jonathan?"

Here came the really tough part. She took a sip from her nearly empty goblet, wishing the table hadn't been cleared. She could use a few French fries to play with. Some ketchup to dip them in.

"What about him?" she asked, needing to hear his concerns before she attempted to tell him what she'd been thinking.

"He just lost his father!" Kip said. "Wouldn't it be cruel to snatch his sister away from him so soon? Without warning? Forever?"

"You think it'd be easier for him to lose her six months from now? Will he love her any less then? Need her any less?"

"No. Of course not."

"I know it's sudden, but there doesn't seem to be a good time to break up the only home they've ever had. And yet, it's going to happen. One way or another. Ada is not their mother and as much as she loves the kids, she's no longer able to raise them. In one sense it seems cruel to prolong this for any of them. Including Ada."

"Jonathan knows something's going on." Kip's words were so soft she barely heard them.

"He said that to you?" She stared at him, finding it difficult to breathe.

Kip nodded. "He's sure I noticed that his skin is a lot darker than his sister's."

"Oh."

"At the same time, he was quick to point out that other than her hair, Kayla looks pretty much like us and he asked me if I thought there was any chance you or your mother would take her. He wanted me to know that he didn't have to come along if that would hurt her chances any."

Tears sprang to Leslie's eyes and she didn't even try to hide them. "What did you say?" she whispered.

"I told him you and your mother are good people and that the color of his or Kayla's skin would not make any difference to you at all. And I told him I liked his hair because it reminded me of his dad, whom I miss very much."

She wiped at the tears sliding down her cheeks. "And you think you aren't father material?" she asked him before she remembered she wasn't going to say anything he might construe as pressure to take custody of her nephew. An unwanted guardianship wouldn't be fair to him, or to Jonathan.

"I have no idea where the words came from," Kip said.

Silence fell for a moment. The bell over the door tinkled again and a man in his early twenties, wearing jeans and a black parka, took a seat at the bar. If he was looking for some action, he'd come to the wrong place.

"My home is…impersonal," Kip said next. "Decorated by a professional, cleaned once a week by a professional."

Was he considering this, then? Her heart pounded heavily.

"I hardly think a child's happiness would be irreparably damaged by either of those factors."

"It's in a gated community that doesn't allow children."

Well, that could present a problem.

"Kip?" She wasn't ready for this. But then, she'd hardly been ready for most of the big events in her life. Starting with her father's death.

He glanced up at her, his brows raised. He wasn't classically handsome, but there was something about Kip that had captured her heart at twelve or thirteen and pretty much never let go.

Not that she was the only girl whose heart had been affected by him. Kip's list of women could rival that of Hawkeye Pierce from all the MASH reruns she used to watch when her roommates were out partying. An especially exciting weekend for her was those thirty-six-hour MASH marathons a local cable station used to run.

"I've been thinking…."

He took a sip of what had to be warm beer. "What?"

"I'd like us to talk to Jim Brackerfield. Find out if I can take both kids. I mean surely…" When it looked like he might interrupt, she rushed on. "If Cal gave me Kayla, the court would acknowledge that he found me a suitable parent."

"He gave you a little girl."

"I hadn't pegged you for a sexist, Kip Webster."

"I'm not," he said, scaring her with his seriousness. Things would go much easier for her if she had his cooperation on this.

"Mothers raise boys all the time," she reminded him.

"Cal grew up without a father." Kip's voice had lost all compromise. She didn't recognize this adamant, straight-faced man. "It was hard on him. A lot harder than you probably know," he continued.

She'd bet her life he was wrong on that one.

"He doesn't want that for his son."

"Surely he'd prefer it to foster care."

He motioned for another round of drinks, waiting while their glasses were removed and replaced. Then, after a long swallow, he continued.

"I did some reading on the Internet this afternoon."

He'd been in her mother's home office when she'd come down from speaking with Nancy.

"Like you said before, one of the most dangerous, life-damaging challenges biracial children face is a sense of not belonging anywhere. They're often unable to feel completely part of one culture or the other. They can suffer terrible insecurities and even self-loathing that sometimes leads to a life of bitterness. Their belief systems can be shakier. I mean, think of it..." He paused for a second and Leslie stared at him. She'd thought about all of this in the past twenty-four hours, of course, but hadn't worked out how to handle these challenges.

Cal's children were just that. Children. Her dead brother's children. Her niece and nephew who needed love. Not black. Not white. Not mixed race. Just *children*.

"...who are they on Martin Luther King day?" he continued after another sip of beer. "One of the people still fighting for equal rights, avenging their forefathers? Or one of those—like you and me—white race who feel guilt for the actions of people who lived before us, people whose actions were completely separate from us and over which we had no control?"

"I don't know." They were children. First and foremost. They needed a home. Security. Love. It was all she could take on at the moment. "You make it sound so hopeless."

"It's not hopeless." He reached across the table, took her hand. "In all the accounts that I read today— and I read about a hundred firsthand accounts on some blogs I found—the insecurities commonly felt by children of mixed heritage can be effectively counteracted within a strong family unit."

Did that mean he wouldn't fight her if she tried to keep Jonathan out of foster care? Reading him as though he were an important investor, Leslie remained quiet. Waiting.

Or maybe she was just too scared to speak.

"I…" He stopped, glanced at her, and she almost started to cry again when she saw his obvious emotional struggle. "I find that I can't turn my back on them, either."

CHAPTER FIVE

THE WORDS WERE the last thing Leslie had expected—at least once she'd prepared herself to take this on all by herself, even though she had no idea how she'd pull it off. She'd been afraid to hope for anything different, had had to convince herself that going it alone was best....

"You aren't saying anything."

"I don't know what to say."

"You don't want me to take Jonathan?" he asked.

The honest doubt in his eyes tore at her. "Of course I do!" she said, only then realizing he was still holding her hand. She gave his fingers a squeeze. "I'm just speechless. Relieved. Thrilled. I've spent the past eight hours trying to figure out how I was going to handle all of this alone...."

Kip sat back. Withdrew his hand to pick up his beer mug. "I'm not so sure I'll be much help."

"Just knowing that Jonathan's being cared for, loved—"

She broke off when he shook his head.

"Didn't you hear anything I said?" he demanded.

"Of course I did."

"Jonathan needs more than my love, Les, he needs a family unit. A strong family unit. And I don't think anyone would call separating him from his only sibling a way to go about creating a 'strong family unit.'"

She wished she hadn't had any wine. She was struggling to keep up with him. That wasn't typical for her.

"I'm not sure what you're suggesting. You live in Ohio. Your job is here. Mine is in Phoenix."

"Actually…" He sat forward again, both hands around the half-full mug of beer as he gazed at her from lowered lids. "The home office for my business is in Phoenix. I'd already been contemplating a move…."

Her heart began to race. Sporting International. How could she have forgotten, even for a minute? She'd instructed Nancy just that afternoon on the necessary actions to ready themselves for the probable takeover. Would Kip lose his job if that happened?

It wasn't a question she could ask him—the takeover wasn't something she could mention—not to an employee in a management position. Being charged with insider trading was a serious risk, even with a personal conversation if it could be construed as somehow sharing privileged information. She'd spent ten years of her life building a reputation that she wasn't going to damage with a few poorly chosen words.

And really, would it affect their decision tonight if he did lose his job? She couldn't see how. And if he was in Phoenix, she could help him out if he needed her to, help with Jonathan, until he got back on his feet.

"Do you have any idea where in Phoenix you'd live?" she asked him. How long had he been thinking about this? If Cal hadn't died, would he have looked her up when he got to town?

She hated that it mattered.

"That's just it," Kip said, drumming the table with his fingertips, his eyes darting away before coming back to rest on her. He wore that predatory expression she'd seen him bestow on any number of cheerleader types during her growing-up years of unrequited love. "I haven't had any time to think through the details yet," he was saying, "but I believe it would be best if we all lived together...."

Leslie stared at him, horrified, immobile. She finally understood the old cliché about jumping from the frying pan into the fire. She would've preferred to remain ignorant of that particular insight.

"LET'S GET OUT OF HERE," Kip said when his living arrangement suggestion was met with a solid minute of openmouthed silence from his lovely companion. He'd just, for the first time in his life, asked a woman to live with him.

Somehow, whenever he'd pictured this moment,

with anticipation or aversion, it hadn't gone anything like *this*. In all his scripts, the woman had been beside herself with joy. Sometimes she'd cried. Sometimes she'd shrieked and laughed and shouted her acceptance from the nearest rooftop. Sometimes she'd wildly torn off her clothes and launched herself at him with thirsty kisses. Of course, those last scenes had been set in private places.

Kip welcomed the blast of cold air that hit him square in the face as he pushed through the heavy wooden door at the front of the bar, and then stood holding it for Leslie, who was still zipping up the parka she'd borrowed from her mother.

She was a beautiful woman—Leslie, not her mother, although Clara was attractive, too, for a woman of her age. But Leslie… Even after four days in her company, he still wasn't used to looking at his best friend's little sister and seeing this gorgeous and completely grown-up woman.

He had no idea what had happened to Leslie during the past ten years, other than the obvious business successes and the little tidbits Cal had dropped after he'd spoken with her. But whatever it was, it had given her a confidence that was visible in every move she made, her posture, the strong, steady stride that said she always knew where she was going.

They were halfway back to the car and she still hadn't said a word.

"You ever going to speak to me again?" If not, it might make living together a little difficult.

"Eventually." She sounded winded. He suspected it wasn't a result of their brisk pace. "When I'm thinking a little more clearly."

Would a few more minutes in the cold take care of that for her? He needed to get this thing settled before he turned tail and ran—and lived the rest of his life haunted by guilt and regret. Not necessarily in that order.

"Too much wine?" he asked.

She shook her head, veered to miss a young couple more engrossed in plastering their lips together than traversing the sidewalk they were occupying. "Too much to figure out."

That he could understand.

"Which is why it's so important to decide on this now," he told her, cursing himself for his impatience even while he heard himself pressing on. "Once we get some decisions made, clarity will be easier to achieve."

"Well, let's be clear on this," she said, her lips pursed as she turned to look at him. She was cold. Her breath puffed out, pale on the night air. "I will not, cannot, live with you."

A group of obviously drunk college students stumbled out of a bar yelling obscenities into the night just as they were passing by.

Kip increased their pace a bit more. "How can

you be so sure? You don't know anything about how
I live."

"I know you're a playboy, Kip Webster."

He frowned. "And?"

"And?" She stopped, stared at him. "I will not live
in a house with a parade of women coming and going."

"I have never once brought a woman to my home.
We either go to her place, or I get a room in a nice
hotel."

She took the next block silently.

"Not that I'm even considering this idiotic idea,
but just for conversation's sake, you *were* speaking
about a strictly platonic relationship, weren't you?"

If he hadn't had so much riding on this, if his entire life wasn't changing faster than he could keep up
with it, Kip would've found some amusement in that
last comment—be it statement or question, he wasn't
quite sure.

"Of course," he said quickly. "At least…" What?
Why had he just said that?

They'd reached the rental car. He unlocked her
side and held open the door. She stood there, staring
at him, her eyes glittering in the dim lights of the
gravel parking lot.

"At least what?"

He shrugged, wished she'd get in, let him shut the
door and turn on some heat.

"I don't know."

Leslie's frown wasn't encouraging, but she got in the car. He'd have to be very careful not to make mistakes like that again.

LESLIE HOPED she made it home without throwing up. The wine and sandwich weren't the problem as much as the conversation. She already had enough to contemplate, an entire new way of life being thrust upon her, without Kip pushing issues that were best left alone.

Vacillating between deep breathing to calm the panic, searching for different perceptions to allay the fear, and reminding herself that she always had a choice and that she was worthy of joy, she'd managed to tie her stomach in knots.

Heat blew out of the vents pointing straight at her. The hot air didn't help. Kip didn't seem to notice the intrusive blast in his face as he turned on to 71, which would take them most of the way back to her mother's house.

"At least what?" For a guy who'd said he wanted to talk, he was being annoyingly silent.

He glanced at her, his face nothing but shadows in the darkened car. At eleven o'clock, there were very few oncoming headlights to illuminate them.

"I…" He sighed, let one hand fall from the steering wheel to his lap. "It's just that we're making so many life-altering decisions in such a short time. Who knows what the future's going to bring as far as our relationship's concerned?"

"I have a different view of relationships than you do. I'm not interested in casual sex."

"I've known you most of your life, Les. I already know that."

Ironically, although he'd given her the acknowledgement she'd been seeking, his words stung. "You don't know what I've been up to during the past ten years. I could've changed."

He glanced at her again, and while she couldn't see the expression in his eyes, she could feel its penetration. "Have you?"

Yes was on the tip of her tongue. Stupid, considering she'd started this whole thing by saying she wasn't that kind of woman. "No."

"Feel better now?"

Not in the least. If anything, she felt worse. Rolling down her window, she sucked in the cold night air.

He was right. It would be cruel to separate Jonathan and Kayla. They were children. Their security and well-being had to come first. If she was certain about nothing else, she knew that. It was a life lesson she'd learned the hard way.

"Why don't you tell me what you envision," she said, pretending for all she was worth that she was in a board room, putting together a billion-dollar deal.

"With the living arrangement, you mean?"

Did he have to spell it out quite so baldly?

Leslie nodded. And then, realizing he couldn't possibly have seen that, said, "Yes."

"I haven't had time to envision much of anything," he told her. "Is your place large enough for all of us?"

She opened her mouth to answer that, but he continued without giving her a chance.

"Do we need to find another place? Put it in both our names?"

This time, Leslie realized that the question was rhetorical.

"That would probably be best." His words just kept right on coming. "We might need to stay at your place for the time being, or maybe you and the kids can stay there and I'll bunk in a hotel if your house isn't big enough, but eventually we'll need a place we both own."

He sounded so certain about that, she just had to ask. "Why?"

"If anything happens to me, everything I have will be Jonathan's. I want to be able to leave him as much security as possible. Same goes for Kayla. I imagine that you'd leave whatever you have to her if something were to happen to you."

If Leslie hadn't already been half in love with the man, she might've fallen for him then.

"Not that I'm agreeing to this, mind you, not at all, but aren't you worried about how it'll look, for the kids' sake? Us living together without being married?"

"Their own parents weren't married."

"But they weren't living together, either."

"Let's cross that bridge when we come to it, okay?"

She couldn't. "I'm not going to marry you, Kip."

"I'm not asking you to marry me, Leslie."

And then something else occurred to her. "What if you want to marry someone else someday?" Or, miracle of miracles, she did.

"What if one of us gets hit by a car?" His response was immediate. "Who knows what the future will bring, Les? We'll deal with it when we have to."

"But…"

"The kids will come first," he said, his voice resonating with complete conviction. "If Jonathan's off at college and Kayla's a perfectly well-adjusted high school student and cool with whatever we decide, and one or the other of us wants to get married, then I guess we could consider it."

His words could not make sense. They could not comfort her or give her hope. There were dangers he didn't know about, dangers that might escalate for her, jeopardizing her hard-won peace, he would be so close, a daily reminder of things she tried to forget.

"What if you fall hopelessly in love?" she asked him. "Are you going to put your life on hold until Jonathan leaves home?"

"Isn't that kind of what we're both agreeing to by taking them in?"

Well, for her, of course, but… "When it comes to women, you don't always think with your…um… brain."

"I'll let that go, Les, because I know you're over-whelmed, but just a note for the future—I don't like to be insulted." His tone was light, easy. It looked like he was grinning.

And Leslie felt the message in her heart. The brash, loud, wild, lost boy might have grown up, but he still craved respect. She wasn't the only one with childhood wounds.

"Point taken." Her response was as lighthearted as his.

"If I take Jonathan, I'm in for the long haul," he said now, his expression completely serious again. "You have my word on that."

She nodded, even though he couldn't see. Watched as the red lights of the car in front of them grew dimmer. The guy had to be doing ninety. At least.

"Back to your little fantasy," she said when the silence began getting on her nerves. "How do you propose we make this work? We split all living expenses, including groceries, divvy up the chores and each support our own kid?"

Not that she'd given it any thought. She was simply hypothesizing.

"The kids' support comes out of a joint fund we both have to sign off on," he reminded her. "Technically we could take some of the living expense money from there, as well."

"I'd rather not," she told him. "I can certainly afford to provide food and shelter, and I'd rather Kayla had the money later, for college, or to open a business."

"I've already decided the same for Jonathan."

Funny how, even in a couple of hours' time, in the midst of drastic change, some decisions just seemed right.

KIP TURNED OFF THE EXPRESSWAY, wishing he had another half hour in the car with Leslie instead of the five minutes it would take to get to her mother's house. He let up on the gas.

"To answer your question, yes, I supposed we'd share living expenses and chores," he said. "I had some vague idea of two suites on opposite ends of the house, with the kids' rooms in between."

He couldn't tell if her silence denoted agreement or disapproval.

"How healthy is it going to be for the kids to see us dating other people?"

"You're really hung up on the dating thing, Les. You said you didn't have a boyfriend. Were you lying about that?"

"No!" She sat up straight, rigid. "I just don't want Jonathan to get the wrong idea with a parade of women in and out of your life."

"He won't see them." He couldn't even think about his sex life at a time like this. Had no idea how things would go. But he knew that whatever it was, his new son was not going to be privy to anything that didn't smack of family wholesomeness—even if it was untraditional family wholesomeness.

"And if you told me you were going to be home, I'd expect you to be there, even if some lovely lady showed up—"

"Leslie!" He stopped the car in front of her mother's house, shifted it roughly into park. "What *is* it with you and my sex life all of a sudden? I thought you wanted me to take Jonathan. Now you think I'm not good enough?"

She stared directly ahead, her chin jutting out. "I *do* want you to take him! And I know you're good enough. It's just that I also know about you and your women," she said. "If we were sharing a house, there'd be a lot of potential problems with—"

"You can't possibly know," Kip told her. "You haven't seen me in ten years, remember?"

"You love women, Kip. That doesn't change."

"I do love women," he said without a hint of guilt or apology, "and I appreciate everything about them. But I also know when and how to exercise that appreciation."

She didn't reply. Probably didn't believe him. Kip sighed. He made a rapid decision that might've been different if he hadn't had those beers, or lost his best friend less than a week before, or been contemplating becoming a father the very next day.

"What did Cal tell you about my father?" he asked her. He'd left the car running for heat. She hadn't reached for the door handle, which meant he still had her attention. She was choosing to continue this conversation.

"I know he wasn't around very often. That he gave you anything you wanted in the way of money or possessions and not much else," she said slowly. "I know he missed every single football game you ever played and that he was in Paris the night of your high school graduation."

All true. All water under the bridge.

"He wasn't always gone," Kip told her. "As a matter of fact, he wasn't away nearly as much as I said he was…"

She'd turned in her seat. He could feel her gaze on him. Kip stared out the front of the windshield, studying the shadows cast by the moon. The bare branches of the huge oak tree in Clara's yard swayed eerily.

"My father enjoyed sex." He searched for words that could convey what he was trying to say without sounding vile. "But he didn't respect women."

There, did that do it? He glanced over at her. Her face was still turned in his direction, but she said nothing, as though waiting for more.

"He was into everything kinky he could find," Kip said. "Pornography, ménage à trois, toys, parties. Women were there for his use. He paid them handsomely and treated them as though they were little more than the bottles that held his whiskey."

"I'm sorry." Her words were a whisper in the darkness.

"For my thirteenth birthday, he bought me a couple of whores. Not just one, which was twisted enough, but two."

CHAPTER SIX

Leslie's eyes were glistening in the darkness. At least she hadn't left the car as he'd half expected her to do. In some respects, Leslie was still so innocent.

"It's amazing you turned out as healthy as you did," she said.

"Your brother and your mother, mostly your brother, were the ones who taught me to see things another way." Kip admitted something he'd never before put in to words. "Cal cherished you and your mom. When he spoke of either of you, it was always with deference, as though you were more precious than gold. No matter how mad he'd get when your mother put her foot down, he'd never speak ill of her. And you…"

Something across the street seemed to have caught her attention.

"You were a kid sister, underfoot, but I never once heard him complain about you or make fun of you."

Her posture didn't change, didn't soften. She didn't move at all.

"And he had that same attitude toward his dates,"

Kip went on, wishing he knew how to help her deal with Cal's death without causing her further pain. "He'd never talk about having sex with his dates—even when the guys teased him about not getting any. He wouldn't even listen if I started in about some hot time I'd had. He'd tell me I was disgusting, that sex was meant to be a private, intimate communication between two people who loved each other. Period. Part of me hated what my father was, but I was young, horny, I knew no other way."

Her hand fell to the armrest above the door handle, but she didn't open the door. Did she want to hear this?

Why did he so badly want to tell her?

Maybe because he'd just lost his best friend and she was that friend's kid sister.

"And then one summer night, between our freshman and sophomore years at college, I talked Cal into driving out to Alum Creek."

It had been a favorite hangout, fishing hole, dope-smoking getaway when he'd been much younger.

"After a couple of beers, Cal told me about this girl he'd been sleeping with. Sounded like it'd been going on for a while. He said that when he was with her, everything inside of him settled and went wild at the same time. He felt safe, alive—and, corny though it sounds, as if he'd found his true home."

Leslie's funny little cough stopped him. He was embarrassing her.

"Apparently this had been going on all through

high school, but when he came back for the summer, she wasn't interested," Kip said and then finally got to his reason for mentioning this at all. "What I remember most about that night is the tone of Cal's voice. He spoke of this girl, being with her, as though he'd found some perfect happiness. It wasn't like any sex I'd ever experienced. And I wanted it."

He felt her stiffen beside him and paused, waiting for her to speak, to tell him this was none of her business, to get out of the car.

"And you know why he had it?"

Her head turned sharply and she stared at him before shaking her head, once.

"Because he respected women. They were people to him, not just there for his pleasure. From that moment on, I've seen women in an entirely different light. I enjoy them. Not only their bodies, but their thoughts, their emotions, their vastly different perspectives."

She bit her lower lip and Kip hoped that he'd just scored at least a small point with her. He meant what he was saying, and he wanted her to believe him.

"I made a vow that night that I would never, ever sleep with a woman just to have sex, I would never kiss and tell, and I would always observe any boundaries set by the women I was involved with. I've never once veered from those rules. Nor will I."

Leslie nodded, blinking as though to get rid of tears. "I won't speak of this again," she said, her voice thick.

Obviously his mention of Cal's lesson had been tough on her. Kip didn't know whether it was best not to mention her brother at all, or to go on remembering. He wasn't up on grief therapy. Before now, he'd never lost anyone he cared about enough to grieve over.

He'd just lost his best friend and was having difficulty with that. Leslie's bereavement was much more intense. She'd not only lost her sibling, but her mentor, her protector, as well.

Which was another reason he had to take little Jonathan. He couldn't leave Leslie to handle this all alone.

"I LIVE IN A FIVE-BEDROOM 3600-square-foot home in a gated community up in the mountains east of Phoenix." With the crazy housing market in Phoenix, houses appreciating as much as $100,000 a year, the place had been too good an investment to pass up.

"Does that fact that you're telling me this mean you're considering my proposal?"

It was late, almost midnight. She was aware that they should go in. Clara would've heard the car pull up. Still, if he was going to take Jonathan, he should know where Kayla would be.

And she had to think about Kayla. Nothing else. She couldn't actually consider his suggestion that they live together, could she? For her, such an arrangement could only be emotional suicide.

"It has a dual master floor plan, which is found

more than not in new Phoenix houses these days." She continued as though she hadn't heard him. If she ignored the question, it might go away.

"With bedrooms in between?"

She nodded.

"What else?"

"I have a lap pool and Jacuzzi in the back, but it's fenced separately from the rest of the yard. I'll put a lock on that gate until Kayla's a little older."

"You live there alone?"

"I had a cat. She died a few months ago." His earlier words were there, distracting her with their threat of things too difficult to manage.

"Les?" Her heart lurched when he laid a hand on her shoulder and used his fingers to turn her head toward him. "Are you inviting Jonathan and me to share this paragon of a home with you?"

"The community has a PGA-approved golf course and state-of-the-art 40,000-square-foot community center." She knew she must sound like a real estate agent, but couldn't seem to stop as she went on listing details. "They do all kinds of programs and have Easter egg hunts and other activities for children throughout the year."

"Les…"

"There are several parks in the neighborhood, as well. A big dog park and a little dog park—for big dogs and little dogs, not a big park and a little park…"

She could see herself staring at him, wanted to

stop. Be aloof. Confident. She licked her lips. Couldn't swallow because her throat was too dry.

"Can you refinance to put my name on the deed?"

Using the shake of her head as an opportunity to look away from him, Leslie stared out the window at the darkened neighborhood of her growing-up years. The houses were older, some with different owners, but still nice. The memories were mixed, some good, some bad. She shook her head again. "I can't."

"Why not?"

She hesitated, but in the end, she simply said, "I own it free and clear."

Kip shifted, but his restlessness felt more like anticipation than impatience. "Will you let me write you a check for half of it?"

"That would be a quarter of a million dollars."

"I have it."

Could she not get a break anywhere?

Across the street the lights behind the curtains in the front room went out. In a minute or so they'd go on upstairs—the front left bedroom. The McCulloughs had had the same nightly routine for thirty years—or as much of those years as Leslie could remember. She'd been shocked at Cal's funeral by how old they'd looked.

"What about kids of your own?" She hadn't meant to ask him that. She wasn't sure the question was really for him.

"What about them?" His voice seemed loud in the quiet night.

"When will you have them?"

"Looking into the future again, Les? Borrowing trouble before it's here?"

"I call it being responsible, considering the consequences of my actions, planning." She used every mental tool she'd learned to keep the defensiveness out of her tone, and was afraid she'd failed, anyway.

He was quiet for a while, leaving Leslie to thoughts she'd prefer to avoid.

"I'd forgotten about your plan to have children of your own." His words, when they finally came, weren't what she'd expected. Or wanted.

"I wasn't talking about me." She said the words too fast. She'd better just give up for the night, go to bed, face life again tomorrow.

"Can we leave that one open for now?" he said, apparently ignoring her assertion. "When you meet the future father of your children, we'll take a look at our circumstances, the kids and where they're at, and go from there, okay?"

She didn't like that at all.

"We'll be different people then, Les, and the answers that are difficult for us now might be perfectly clear."

Oh. The knots in Leslie's stomach loosened slightly. Had he actually come up with something that made sense? It was a relief after more than an hour of talk about living together.

Her stomach jumped with some other emotion. Dread? Fear? Exhaustion. She was a basket case bordering on hopeless. Juliet would be shaking her head.

But she wouldn't be disappointed. Her counselor would confirm that Leslie had done her best. She didn't have anything to be ashamed of. She wasn't responsible for the choices of others.

She almost grinned when thoughts of the other woman brought to mind the reassurances—the truths—that had saved her from a life of getting through each day trying not to have an "episode." Panic attacks brought on by feelings of unworthiness, Juliet would say. Unnecessary feelings. Unjustifiable ones.

"You grew up without a father." Kip's voice was so soft she shivered in spite of the warmth of the car. "I grew up without a mother. We both suffered for it."

He had no idea how much.

"Is that what we want for these kids?"

"No." He had her there.

"I THINK IT WOULD BE BEST if I took Kayla to Phoenix first."

It was three o'clock in the morning and Kip was still wide awake, if numb and thick-headed with exhaustion, as he sat with Leslie at her mother's kitchen table, drinking a cup of decaffeinated coffee.

Clara had gone up to bed an hour before—after hearing about their plans—and crying tears of relief.

And shocking them with her sudden decision to move to Phoenix, leaving behind sixty years of life and history and friends in Columbus. Her grandchildren came first.

"And you're both going to need my help…" she'd said when they'd tried to talk her out of such a drastic move.

Truthfully, Kip had been more relieved than anything to know that Clara would be close.

It would be good for them. He had a feeling there were a million things he and Leslie didn't know about being parents—and it wasn't like they were going to have the infant months as a training period. No, they'd be thrown into this without any chance to get used to their new reality first.

But it would be good for him in another way, as well. He could watch out for her, be there to help with the little things Cal had always done, if she was close by.

Leslie was watching him, her eyes filled with compassion. "Did you hear anything I just said?"

He frowned. "That you're going to take Kayla first," he remembered. And then, realizing there was more, he grimaced. "Sorry."

Her smile gave him an uneasy moment. He was going to be living with that, and he liked it a little too much. He was reminded of a show he'd watched as a kid—*Lost in Space,* he thought the name was. What he remembered was a robot that was constantly wagging its arms while issuing a warning. "Danger! Danger! Danger!"

"You're exhausted, Kip. Why don't you go to bed? We can finish this in the morning."

He sat up. Took a sip of coffee that had grown lukewarm. "I'm fine," he said. "I'll sleep better once we have a plan." It was true. "And I suspect you will, too."

If he'd learned nothing else about the grown-up Leslie, he knew that having a plan was about as important to her as breathing.

"Okay." She rose, brought their cups over to the sink and rinsed them. Then she poured two glasses of ice water, using her mother's oversize crystal goblets.

"Sorry, this is all that was handy," she said, referring to the water as she set a wine goblet in front of him. "But it should help in the sleep department since it's not caffeine."

Kip was willing to accept any assistance. He wasn't relishing the moment he'd finally be alone in the dark with nothing but his own thoughts for company. He had a feeling there were some heavy-duty admonishments waiting for him.

"So tell me again what you said about taking Kayla."

"Only that I'm ready to leave tomorrow. And I think it'd be good for Kayla if she and I have a little time alone so she can get used to me. Same goes for you and Jonathan." She took a sip of her water, her lips full and pink along the rim of the glass.

God, he *was* tired.

"I'm afraid that if we take them together, it could end up being you and me against Jonathan and Kayla—or at least Jonathan and Kayla clinging together instead of opening up to us."

"Makes sense."

"We want them to have a feeling of family, but it seems like it'd be easier to adjust to us one at a time." She paused, frowned. Kip loved how intensely she approached everything she did. It was no surprise she'd been a wonder kid in the finance world.

"We'll tell Jonathan, of course, that he'll be seeing Kayla again very soon—and that he'll be living with her. With us."

He nodded, thanking God for her plans. What had seemed completely impossible moments before had become slightly more manageable.

"The break will give you time to get things arranged here, and also let Jonathan finish the term at school."

Kip glanced up at her, feeling at a complete loss. "I hadn't even thought of that," he admitted. "How'm I doing as a father so far?"

Placing her hand gently over his, Leslie smiled again. "Just fine," she said. "Take a sip of your water."

He did.

And she went to bed.

"NO!" KAYLA STOOD, her plump little body completely naked, in the alcove between the bed and bath in the suite Leslie had given her in Phoenix.

"Come on, sweetie, you're wet. Aunt Leslie doesn't want you to slip and hurt yourself."

"No!" The girl, her dark frizzy hair sticking up like some kind of wild halo, shook her head from side to side.

Leslie stood, empty towel between her hands, afraid to approach the child in case she tried to run— and afraid not to, for a lot of reasons. If she'd thought Kayla would be any good at it, she'd let her be the boss between them, but she knew damn well that would lead them both to disaster.

"Kayla, it wasn't nice to run away from Aunt Leslie."

"Wa wa," the little girl said, glancing at the warm tub Leslie had pulled her out of moments before.

One of the many things she'd learned during the past four days alone with the most contrary angel on the planet was that Kayla liked bathtime. A lot. After the first morning, when the two of them had shown up at day care an hour late with Leslie's hair as frizzy as her new daughter's, Leslie had scheduled evenings for bathtime.

The disadvantage was that the child seemed crankier in the evening. And Leslie was scared to death Kayla would run off, slip, crack her head open.

Leslie would never forgive herself.

"If I let you back in the bath for five minutes, you promise to stand still while I dry you?"

Kayla, brown eyes large and round, nodded.

"Okay," she said, approaching the little girl, afraid she'd spiral away. But Kayla stood completely still. Watching her.

Leslie picked her up.

It was just that easy.

Now if only she had the courage to just dry the little imp and put her to bed without keeping her promise.

But Leslie plopped the slippery body back down in the plastic safety ring suctioned to the bottom of the tub, sitting on the side for added protection.

She hadn't been a parent long enough to feel comfortable exercising subterfuge. Or even knowing how…

SITTING DOWN ON THE COUCH in Juliet's office on Friday at noon, Leslie laid her head back and scowled at the counselor who'd released her from treatment years ago, but who continued to see Leslie once a month anyway, because Leslie wasn't ready to stop visiting with the woman she'd grown so fond of.

"A new necklace," Juliet said from her armchair.

"It was on sale. The notice was one of the nine-hundred messages in my in-box when I got back on Monday. Part of the spring line. Somehow I'd missed it."

"Glad to see you ordered it immediately," Juliet

said, still looking in apparent admiration at the violet and pink crystals that sparkled from their antique-gold flower settings at the opening of Leslie's cream blouse. She'd chosen her violet suit quite deliberately that morning. Violet was said to bring peace of mind. At least to some people.

"So how're you doing otherwise?" Juliet's casual question belied the compassion in her eyes.

"Good." Since Leslie's regularly scheduled appointment wasn't for another couple of weeks, she'd called Juliet on Monday to ask for this meeting. And she'd told her everything that had happened in her life, prompting the call.

"Hey," Juliet said, grinning. "that makes this the quickest meeting we've ever had…."

"Okay, not that great," Leslie admitted, grinning in response. "I'm…managing." It was a word Juliet was fond of.

"Finding that you're a new mother—of a two-year-old—is a harrowing experience no matter who you are," Juliet told her with enough calm to convince Leslie that she was perfectly normal. At that moment, anyway. "You'll adjust."

She nodded. Juliet might be right. But the verdict was still out.

The night before, Kayla had spent an extra half hour in the bath, not the agreed-upon five minutes. And then she'd still tried to run from Leslie, who'd carried her, kicking and screaming, into the bedroom and placed her on the dresser to dry her.

"The furniture I bought for Kayla is being delivered tomorrow. I sure will be glad to have a bed with side-bars so I don't have to worry about her falling out."

"You ordered a junior bed?"

"It's a regular-size twin, with removable safety bars." She'd thought about ordering one for Jonathan, too, until she'd realized he was far too old to need the bars.

And Jonathan's possessions were Kip's concern.

CHAPTER SEVEN

"So HAVE YOU HEARD from Kip since you've been back?"

Even after all these years, it disconcerted her when Juliet appeared to read her mind.

"Every night," she said quickly before Juliet did any more mind-reading.

"And?"

"I'm scared to death, Juliet," she said, lifting her head.

"Is there any particular reason, or is this just a general, resistance-to-change fear?"

"I'm afraid…" She couldn't say it. Couldn't admit, even to herself, that she might be in much bigger trouble than anyone suspected. "I'm afraid of all kinds of things. Having a little girl in my life—my house—is enough of an adjustment, but a grown man?"

"It could be good."

"How?"

"You were in danger of becoming too comfortable, Leslie. You'd bought that big house, made it completely your own, and before you knew it, your life was settling into a predictable pattern."

"Living alone isn't a bad thing."

"It is if you don't want to spend your life alone—and you don't. And it's particularly a concern if you're someone with a goal of motherhood. Your living situation was counterproductive to your goal. Funny how the universe has a way of taking care of things for us sometimes when we're too dense to see them for ourselves."

How did Juliet always make the impossible seem almost sane?

"Even if I could've seen this one coming, I wouldn't have chosen it." Leslie couldn't resist the sardonic reply. And then she couldn't resist crossing her fingers where they lay on the couch cushion. Just in case this was going to work, she didn't want to jinx herself.

"You're doing okay with Kayla, you've got Kip and Jonathan's arrival during the Christmas break all planned, he'll have his own suite on the other side of the house, chores are divided...."

Juliet had paid a lot of attention to that call on Monday. Leslie nodded as she paused.

"...so what's the *real* problem?"

"I—"

Juliet lowered her chin, glancing at Leslie over the top of her glasses. "Yes?"

"I'm... I don't know... When he calls—" Thank

God her business associates couldn't see her now, stumbling over her words like some flustered nincompoop. "I— My stomach kind of jumps, you know?"

She was shocked when Juliet actually laughed. "Yeah?"

"Yeah. So…what's that about?"

"You're attracted to him."

"No, I'm not." She couldn't be. Not now, as an adult. "I mean, I was when I was a kid, but that was a long time ago."

"Apparently you still are."

Sure, she'd noticed that Kip was as attractive as he'd always been, but not in any way that affected her personally. Or at least not once she'd recovered from that first unexpected meeting two weeks before. She couldn't feel any real desire for him. It would be too messy…too…

She just couldn't. That was all. There were some things even Juliet didn't know. And that was how it had to be. Juliet had helped her heal so she wouldn't have to go back to that part of her life.

And she wasn't going to.

Ever.

LESLIE HUNG UP the phone with one of her largest investors late Friday afternoon, after assuring him that although Sporting International hadn't gone public as soon as expected, she was still confident it would. She'd been poring over the stats all week and knew that something had to happen within the next month or the company would go under. The issue was cash flow. SI was struggling to find extra capital to open stores rapidly enough to keep up with the competition. She was working from facts, but also from intuition—she had a hunch. The moment she'd started "listening" to those hunches in her first job out of college, she'd become an overnight success.

She looked up from the piles of papers on her desk—there were always several big deals in the works—as the brief rap that always preceded Nancy's arrival was followed by the appearance of her frowning face.

"What is it, Nance?" she asked, hoping that whatever the problem was, it wasn't too big. Or could be put off until Monday. With the pressing work in front of her, she'd be in the office until eight o'clock that night.

And the day care closed at five.

"Rumor has it that SI just sold to a private investor."

Leslie froze, her pen poised above the notepad. "How solid is the rumor?"

"Ely." Nancy named the security officer at one of Phoenix's most upscale investment outfits. He played hunches mixed with fact almost as well as Leslie did. And he was privy to a different set of facts.

"Move everything over to Reynolds," she said, mentally calculating who she'd call first to maximize damage control. Most of her larger clients socialized in the same circles. And this was Friday night. Reynolds Electric was definitely going public the following week. The payout wouldn't be as big as SI would've been, and it wouldn't happen as fast, but long term, it would be a good investment. Decent enough for her to save face and buy time to discover the next big find.

Or so she told the knot in her stomach.

"I just can't figure it out," she said, as Nancy didn't immediately scurry to do her bidding but stood there watching her with that worried-mother look. "A private investor. There wasn't one single hint that amounted to anything."

"Ely seemed to think it was from within."

"I went over their employee list." She remembered the night quite clearly. She'd been alone in the office—in the entire building—late one Saturday night a couple of months before. She'd come from a black-tie charity affair, where she'd had one glass of wine to get her through until she could leave without offending any of her dozen or so clients who were in attendance. That was the night she'd discovered that Kip Webster had risen to vice president of sales in the growing company. "I didn't see anyone on it with that kind of capital."

"Just proves that money doesn't always show." Nancy echoed one of Leslie's oft-repeated phrases.

And still the older woman didn't leave. Nancy had some quick work to do—and Leslie was impatient to get to her phone calls before she had to collect Kayla.

"The little girl," Nancy said, not quite meeting Leslie's gaze.

"Yes?"

"She has African-American hair."

"Her mother was African-American."

Nancy nodded, her lower lip pushed up in contemplation.

"And the little boy who's coming to live with you," Nancy continued. "He's African-American, too?"

"And half white. Like his sister."

"You said your brother's best friend was moving into the other side of your house to raise the boy."

"That's right."

"That wouldn't happen to be the same young man from SI who was here last week, would it?"

"Yes," Leslie said, frowning. "Why?"

"Because I think they're here."

"What?" Leslie jumped up. "He's not due until next week! I'm not ready for him. I—" She stopped abruptly when she noticed the surprise—and then the smile—on Nancy's face at her uncharacteristic outburst.

"So it's that way, is it?" the older woman murmured.

As Leslie started to refute the erroneous conclusions her secretary was drawing, Nancy went right on speaking.

"It's about time."

About time for what? To get herself a new secretary?

And counselor, too?

"What did you mean you think they're here?" she asked, refusing to look in the mirror, to check her fly-away curls and the state of her make-up, with the older woman looking on. Judging her.

"I saw them downstairs, heading for the day care, when I was coming up from the mailroom."

Leslie had to glance in the mirror, after all, then smoothed her hair behind her ear, and moved toward the door.

"I wish you'd said something sooner...." She pulled open the door just in time to see Kip and Jonathan enter the outer office of her suite.

"I thought the SI deal was the bigger news...."

She barely registered Nancy's not so lightly uttered words as Jonathan walked purposefully toward her.

"They wouldn't let us take Kayla." He was clearly disgusted. Just as clear was the fact that he held her somehow responsible.

Leslie looked from him to Kip, and quickly back. The angry young boy she wanted so desperately to please was the least of the problems confronting her. It had only been five days since she'd seen Kip and the sight of him, there in the flesh, had her heart racing.

She knelt down by the dark-skinned little boy with dark red curls just like her brother's. "It's to keep her safe, honey," she said. "They don't know you yet and they won't let her go with anyone I haven't signed her out to. That way someone bad can't just walk off with her."

"I'm her brother." Jonathan so obviously wanted to sound strong. Commanding. She had a feeling he wouldn't be at all pleased to know that she could hear the tears in his voice.

"And we'll tell them that, right now," she said, standing. She held out her hand to him. "Come with me."

"What about the phone calls?" Nancy asked. "Hi," she said to Jonathan. "I'm Nancy."

Introductions were exchanged. "I'll make the calls as soon as I get back," Leslie said, and then met Kip's gaze head on for the first time since he'd come in.

"If I give you a key to my place, would you mind taking Kayla and Jonathan home? I had a big deal fall through half an hour ago and I've got a couple of hours of work...."

"Of course," Kip said, reaching for the elevator button as they approached. "We'll go to a drive-through for hamburgers and french fries and watch some TV. I imagine you have a television?"

"Fifty-inch," Leslie said. "In the family room. Remote's in the drawer by the couch."

She could work until eight. Or nine or ten. Even though the day care was closing in an hour.

And for the first time since this whole nightmare began, she could see the benefit in having Kip Webster as a roommate.

"I HAVE A FEELING it's way past your sister's bedtime, buddy," Kip said sometime after nine that evening, turning off the Disney show Jonathan had been watching. Kayla was lying on the floor beside him, head tilted toward the television, thumb in her mouth.

"She can't go yet."

It hadn't taken long for Jonathan's wide-eyed stare to win him over for good. About a minute actually— the moment he'd walked the little boy from Ada King's home and saw him struggling not to cry.

He'd taught his first father-son lesson right there in the condominium parking lot. Boys could cry if they needed to. They just did it and got it done.

Jonathan had. Holding the child against him in the front seat of the car, feeling the sobs wracking the small body, listening while Jonathan told him all the reasons he *didn't* need to cry, he'd given his heart to someone other than a woman for the first time in his adult life.

"What do you mean she can't go yet?" he asked the boy now. Kayla, eyes half-closed, looked from her brother to him.

"She needs her diaper changed."

He'd been wondering about that. Truth be known, it was the reason he'd held off this long in putting the kids to bed. He'd been hoping for Leslie to show up and rescue him.

"I think between the two of us we can handle that," he told the boy with a lot more confidence than he felt.

He'd never changed a diaper in his life. Wasn't even sure how to begin. He'd spent the past half hour hoping that Leslie was using those tape things he'd seen advertised on TV rather than the safety pin kind he'd seen on old sitcoms.

Jonathan shook his head, his full lips completely straight as he stared at Kip. "Boys don't never look at little naked girls."

It was the only time, since their first hour together in the parking lot of the condominium, that Jonathan had disagreed with him. At least openly.

Kip was treading on dangerously thin ground here. "Where'd you hear that?" he asked, listening desperately for Leslie's car.

Would she come in through the garage into the kitchen? Or park outside and come in the front door?

"Daddy told me," Jonathan said, standing between Kip and his sister. "He said, Jonathan, boys don't never look at little naked girls."

"This is different, son," Kip said, praying to whatever fate might be willing to have mercy on him for the right words. "You aren't looking at her to see her naked, you're only helping her take care of things she's too little to take care of herself."

How much did five-year-olds know about sex? Or nakedness, for that matter? Weren't little kids oblivious to stuff like that?

"No." Jonathan's tone grew more adamant. He moved closer to his sister, his back to the girl who hadn't moved, other than to turn her head once, since Kip had shut off the television. Hands on his hips, the boy stared hard at Kip.

"Daddies take care of their baby daughters all the time, Jonathan." *Come on, Les, I need you here.* "I'm sure your dad helped change Kayla's diapers, gave her baths."

"No, he didn't." Jonathan's expression was solemn. He wasn't giving an inch. "Daddy didn't never do that. He said it was woman's work."

"Your father was the furthest thing from a chauvinist," Kip said. And then, at Jonathan's blank stare, tried again. "He did whatever chores were necessary." Kip couldn't remember a time he'd felt so inept. "He used to help his mom with the dishes, and..." A lightbulb went off. "He took care of his little sister, too, after their father died and their mother had to work."

"Daddy's sister...Aunt Leslie—" he said the name slowly, as though just getting used to it "—was nine when their daddy died. Daddy told me. She was all growed up a lot bigger than Kayla *and* me." The boy frowned. "You can't change her diaper, Uncle Kip," he insisted again. "Daddy said so."

Kip was getting nowhere. And no new ideas were presenting themselves.

"Come on, Jonathan," he said. "Think back to when Ada was busy and your daddy was looking after you. You can't remember one time he changed Kayla?"

The boy shook his head. "He always waited for Ada and made me and him go away and close the door so Kayla wouldn't be 'barrassed and cry. He said so."

The boy was obviously wrong, but Kip didn't have any way to help him understand that. He glanced around Jonathan's shoulder.

"She's asleep."

Jonathan took a quick look behind him. "Yep."

"How about if we put her to bed in her overalls and wait for Aunt Leslie to change her into her pajamas?"

"Okay."

"Okay."

Sliding his arms gently beneath the sleeping toddler, Kip carried her upstairs, hoping Leslie didn't plan to work late again until her charge was fully grown.

"WHAT WAS THE BIG DEAL that fell through?"

Although it was almost midnight before Leslie made it home, Kip had been waiting up for her, handing her a glass of wine the minute she walked in.

He'd changed into jeans—and a T-shirt with sleeves that fit his shoulders a little too well. She was having a hard time ignoring them.

"You were probably aware of it before I was," she said, glancing down. His feet were bare.

Leslie knew she was exhausted but felt a surge of

energy anyway. It had to be leftover adrenaline and caffeine from a long night at the office that just kept getting longer.

"How would I have been aware of it?"

Dropping her briefcase, purse and keys on the island in the kitchen, she took the glass of wine and walked through to the family room, expecting chaos.

The room was spotless.

Leslie stood there, surveying her domain, surprised that it looked exactly as it had every other night she'd come home late in the three years since she'd bought the house. Rose-colored sofa, darker rose armchairs, beige hand-woven wool rug with rose and green flowers. Side tables, coffee table, silk flower arrangements, television, entertainment center. Fireplace. Books.

Her surprise was not so much at the appearance of the room, but more at the hint of disappointment it brought.

She'd changed her life. Drastically. That should show, shouldn't it?

"The deal wasn't really a deal," she said slowly, kicking off her violet pumps as she dropped onto the sofa. "It was a hunch I had a lot riding on."

"You do that often?" he asked, a half-empty bottle of beer in hand as he took the chair across from her, bringing those damned shoulders with him.

When she tried to ignore everything but the conversation they were trying to have, questioning his statement with a silently raised brow, he said, "Ride a lot on hunches?"

"Every single day."

He grinned. "I'm impressed."

"Why?" She liked his grin. Because she was so lonely that his smile made a long night seem suddenly enjoyable?

"You're successful at what you do, which means the hunches are good ones. And you have the confidence and courage to follow through. You're not afraid to take risks."

She didn't know about any of *that*. He could very well be putting her on some kind of kid-sister pedestal that was bound to come crashing down.

And probably soon, considering that they were going to be living in the same house, seeing each other every day.

Having breakfast together. Doing the dishes. Grocery shopping. Raising the kids…

Leslie slid out of her jacket. She hadn't noticed it was so hot in here when she'd come in or she would've adjusted the thermostat.

"Anyway, you would have known first because I'm talking about the company you work for. I figured SI for an announcement of going public before the end of the year. I had investors cash in so they'd be ready and waiting to buy in the second that happened."

He took a sip of beer. Watching her. Saying nothing.

"I'm sure you know it's not a company that

would've had people scurrying for stock in the first hour," she told him. "But it's a gold mine of potential. Which made it a guaranteed stock option."

"I'm glad to hear you say that."

"Why?"

"Because I value your opinion."

Something was going on here. She was being slow; she could feel it.

And then she felt her face turn red. "*You* bought the company." Why hadn't she guessed earlier? But last she'd known, Kip's father had squandered away his inheritance. Still, these facts, along with a new hunch, added up. "That's why you were moving to the Phoenix-based headquarters."

He nodded.

"But...how?" she asked, then shook her head at her own social ineptitude. "Sorry. It's none of my business."

"Of course it's your business," he said. "We're living together!"

Her portfolio was none of *his* business. And she wasn't living with him. They were sharing a house. All of which she was too tired to get into that night.

"My father might've thrown away a shitload of money while he was alive, but he also happened to buy into an oil well in Texas—a drunken poker game, so I'm told. Turns out, the land really did have oil. I get dividends every six months. It wasn't enough to buy SI, but it was enough to guarantee the backing to keep it privately held. Of course, if I don't get some stores built and turn things around, I stand to lose everything."

"Wow. *You* own SI." *Intelligent, Les.* She just didn't know what else to say. She had an independently wealthy man, much richer than she was, living under her roof.

Leslie had liked it better when they were equals.

CHAPTER EIGHT

"YOU'LL HAVE the company in the black a year from now."

Kip was exhausted. Needed to go to bed, sleep for about a month. But it had been a long week without her, a long night without quiet time. He wasn't ready to end these moments.

And he needed to talk to her.

"I hope so," he said, leaning forward to put his empty beer bottle down on the coffee table between them. "I had no idea you were on to us," he said, understanding why she hadn't been able to talk about her plans, but regretting the way things had played out anyway. Less than two weeks before he'd vowed to protect her. So far he was doing a bang-up job. "How much damage did I just do?"

And could he undo it?

She took a sip of wine. "Several hours on the phone tonight when I should've been home...." The half smile she sent him was nice. Maybe too nice. "And my promotion to full partner will probably be a little slower."

"Ah, Les." He finished off the bottle of warm beer he'd been nursing for a couple of hours. "I'm sorry."

"I was a little agitated about it earlier," she said, her expression relaxed as she looked him straight in the eye. "But in my business 'easy come, easy go' is the only motto that keeps you sane. One thing I've learned in the past ten years is that there's always another opportunity. Always."

"So now what?"

"I go find it."

He frowned, the guilt spreading through him.

"Lighten up, Webster," she said, smiling again. "I have other deals pending. You didn't break me. I promise."

He couldn't tell how truthful she was being, but he had to admit she didn't appear to be falling apart at the seams. She'd just lost a potential promotion, not to mention a huge amount of money, and she was smiling. He wasn't sure he'd ever met a woman like her.

"So, how were the kids tonight?" She was half-lying in a corner of the couch, her glass of wine resting on her belly—a nicely curved, slender belly.

He'd do better to think about the deal he'd inadvertently cost her.

"They were pretty quiet," he said. "Stayed close together. I offered them some of the toys I found up in Kayla's room, but they weren't interested. I'd guess that once Jonathan's stuff gets here it'll be different."

"This place probably seemed huge to him."

"I would've thought it might seem huge to you, too, living here all alone."

She shrugged. "I didn't plan to always be alone," she said, reminding him of an earlier conversation and her desire to be a mother someday. "And I got in at a rock bottom price before this community was even officially on paper. I knew I couldn't afford to pass up the investment. This is actually one of the smallest homes here."

"It's beautiful, Leslie. You know how to make a place feel warm—welcoming."

She turned away, hugging a hand to her shoulder. "Kayla was awfully happy to see Jonathan this afternoon."

He allowed the memory of the little girl's squeal when she first saw her brother to distract him—as he was sure Leslie had intended. "We made the right choice, deciding to keep them together," he said.

Surely she could see that now?

With a somewhat nervous look in his direction, she glanced down. "It's not them I'm worried about."

Kip stood, moved over to the other end of the couch—into her line of vision. "You have nothing to fear from me, Les, I swear to you."

"I'm not afraid of you."

"What then?"

Leslie sighed, ran a hand through her wild red curls, which made him wonder what that felt like. "The potential," she said eventually.

He frowned. "We've discussed every minute detail, clear down to dating, trash day and R-rated movies on the premises. And we'll continue to discuss them as they come up. I don't see the problem."

Pointing at him and then back at herself she said, "You…me…late nights…conversation…"

"It's my first night in town." Kip quelled the disappointment that flared at her words. Until that very second, this time with her had been the best part of his day. Hell, maybe even his week. "I thought it was the proper thing to wait for you and report in."

She nodded, sipped from her goblet. And then again. "I know," she said. "And I'm glad you did. It's just…"

Kip was content to let that sentence hang there for however long she let it. Her hesitation, her obvious reluctance, shouldn't matter so much, and as soon as he got acclimated, was in his element, it *wouldn't* matter. For tonight, he was glad she was glad.

"It's dangerous, Kip."

He couldn't tell why she was whispering. "How so?" he asked.

"It's—I don't know…intimate."

"Living together is intimate."

"We *aren't* living together. We're sharing a house."

He didn't see the distinction. "You're beginning to make me feel as though I don't belong here." He didn't like the feeling one bit.

"Oh, no!" She set the wineglass down next to his

empty bottle. Leaned toward him. "You do! I…it was the right decision. I really see that. It's just…"

There it was again. That hanging sentence. He was fairly certain he'd rather she left it hanging there indefinitely.

"I…" She licked her lips, stared down at her lap. "I'm afraid we might end up doing something that would…ruin everything."

Understanding brought a mixed bag of emotions, probably made more confusing by his fatigue. He would've preferred to leave the topic for another night—another century. One look at the suddenly tight expression on her face and he knew he had to take part in whatever was coming before he'd be able to sleep.

"You're afraid we might become sexually in-volved." Perverse of him, maybe, to simply lay it out there when everything about her indicated that she wanted to skirt right around this one. Nevertheless, he thought plain speaking would help.

"No!" Her horrified expression shocked him. "I mean…maybe." She'd turned red, picked up her wine, took a gulp.

What the hell was going on?

"If it happens, it happens." He wouldn't mind. She was one of the most beautiful women he'd been around in a long time.

She shook her head, avoiding his gaze. "It can't happen."

"Then it won't."

That got her to look up at him. "You don't know that."

"I know me. If you don't want anything to happen between us, it won't."

He didn't like the smirk on her face. "You're a guy, Kip."

"And your point is?"

"Guys, you know, get carried away, forget to think…."

What the hell kind of men had she been running with? "Some do," he acknowledged. "Decent men don't." He watched her, waiting to make sure he had her complete attention. "I don't."

"Well…"

"Besides," he interrupted, "are you insinuating that women don't get carried away by the moment sometimes?"

"No." She shook her head. "No…I realize they do."

Okay. He was kind of liking this conversation now. "And that's part of the problem?"

Taking her goblet, Leslie jumped up and hurried to the window, pulling aside the closed drape to peer into the night. She lived on over an acre of natural desert, across from a mountain, so he didn't figure there was much she could see out in that blackness.

Instinct told him to go to her, to take her into his arms and promise her that everything would be okay.

Instead he sat and lamented the fact that he didn't have a cold beer in his hand.

Eventually, about the time Kip was ready to say to hell with caution and go to her, she turned.

"I…I…I'm usually pretty articulate…"

Under other circumstances Kip would have grinned. He rubbed his neck. It ached with tension.

Wineglass held inches from her mouth, she started to speak again, then cringed. Kip wasn't sure how much more of this he could take.

"I don't find you unattractive." She let out a huge breath with the last word.

Kip wondered why the admission was so difficult. "Okay."

"But…I can't do it, Kip. I can't have casual sex."

"Who says it would be casual?"

"And what would happen if it ended? How would we continue living together? What about the kids?"

"More borrowing trouble from the future, Les?"

She watched him for a long moment before she shook her head. "I don't think so."

He did.

"I don't know. Wouldn't it be better to have an understanding now, before anything gets out of hand? Then if…something comes up, the decision's already made."

If they'd been discussing what kind of discipline to mete out to the kids, he'd agree with her. "I think decisions of a sexual nature often get changed as the moment warrants."

"I…" Leslie's glass hit the coffee table so hard he was surprised it didn't break. She fell into the armchair he'd vacated, her head in her hands.

"Les? What is it?" He was too tired to be doing this.

She glanced up at him, though she didn't raise her head much. "I like you."

Kip couldn't help grinning as relief replaced some of the tension that had been holding him hostage. Was *that* what this was all about?

"I like you, too."

"I want to *keep* liking you."

"And what makes you think you won't?"

She stood. Moved to the couch. Sat. Then looked him straight in the eye. "Okay. Here it is," she said.

Thank God for that. He hoped.

"What happens if, say, you get the idea one day that I want to be kissed—"

"Then I kiss you."

"No, let me finish…." She frowned at his interruption.

So much for trying to introduce a little levity. Had the woman never heard that sex could be fun? Even in the talking stages? Especially the talking stages?

"Say that happens, which it won't, and it's good…"

So far he wasn't hearing anything that could become a problem.

"…so naturally, you want to take things further," she continued.

Kip nodded.

"And I don't."

He shrugged. "Then we stop."

"Just like that?" Her eyes her wide. How could that have shocked her?

"Of course just like that."

"I say no, at the most inopportune moment, and you just stop." It was a statement, but clearly one she doubted.

"Yes." He wanted there to be no doubt at all.

"And then you lose respect for me, or liking for me, or find me too difficult to be around…."

He wondered again, with a little more emotion attached, what kind of men she'd been with. "No."

"No?" She didn't believe him.

"No." Kip leaned forward until their noses were only inches apart, staring straight at her. "No," he said again. "I'm not some insecure piece of manhood, Les. I can take rejection just fine. In fact, I'd much rather have an honest rejection between us than a pretense of anything else."

"You would." Another statement, but not quite such a disbelieving tone.

"I would."

She thought for several minutes, nodding several times. Then she looked over at him. "Okay."

He was almost too tired to believe his luck. "Okay?"

"For now. I won't borrow trouble from the future on this one."

The relief was heady. Headier than the effects of the beer he'd consumed.

"Does this mean we can go to bed now?" He was grinning as he glanced over at her.

"Bed! Oh my gosh! I forgot! I haven't made up your suite yet…"

Kip put a hand on her arm as she began to jump up. "I already did it," he said. "I figured out pretty easily which room was yours, and which one was Kayla's. So determining that my suite was the master at the other end of the house didn't take long. I found sheets in the linen closet in the bathroom, then Jonathan and I made a game out of bed-making."

"Jonathan's room is ready."

"I know."

Her smile almost had him wishing she'd ask for that kiss. "Are you as tired as I am?" she asked.

Kip nodded, planning to stand. As soon as he found the energy.

"Did Kayla give you any trouble going down?"

Kayla. *Shit*. Kip sat up. He'd forgotten.

"Um, she's not really down yet." He hated to tell her she had more work to do before she could go to bed.

Leslie stood, frowning at him. "What do you mean? She's awake?" She moved toward the hall. "I haven't heard her. Where is she?"

If he'd had any doubt that she already loved this

child with all her heart, she'd just allayed it. "She's asleep," he said, joining her in the hall. "In her bed." They were almost at the door of Kayla's room. "She's still dressed," he continued, lowering his voice to a near whisper, though they were going to be waking the child, anyway, so his care seemed unnecessary.

Would she cry when they woke her?

Thank goodness Jonathan's room was on the other side of the house with his.

As soon as she'd checked the sleeping child, Leslie glanced over her shoulder at him, grinning. "You afraid to tackle the bath?" she asked him.

She'd told him about her nightly ritual—every night when he'd called. By the third night, the first thing he'd asked when she'd answered the phone was how Kayla's bath had gone.

"I wasn't even going to try that," he told her. "But I *was* planning to figure out how to change her diaper and get her into pajamas."

"You haven't changed her diaper?" Leslie looked as though he'd served the children mud for dinner. "Since four o'clock this afternoon?"

"I…"

"She'll get diaper rash, Kip!" She uncovered the little girl gently. "You should've told me you didn't know how. I would've shown you. Or made other arrangements."

"Les." He stopped her before she slid her arms beneath Kayla's shoulders, turning her toward him. "I didn't not change her because I didn't know how. Although that's true, too. I don't know how, but I would've figured it out. I didn't change her because Jonathan refused to allow it."

"What?" She frowned at him. "Why not?"

"He said that Cal told him boys never look at naked little girls. He claims Cal never changed her, either."

She paled. "He said that?"

Kip nodded. Maybe she'd have some idea how to convince Jonathan that he'd misunderstood, that of course fathers tended to their daughters' needs. That it was perfectly right for them to do so.

Leslie turned back to Kayla. "Come on, pumpkin," she said softly, gently pulling at the snaps in the legs of Kayla's overalls. "Let's get you more comfortable."

Kayla didn't seem to mind the cooler air on her skin, sleeping on as Leslie tended to her.

"Would you bring me a diaper?" she asked Kip. "They're in that white thing hanging on the closet door."

He hurried over.

"And a wet wipe, too?" she asked. "They're in the top dresser drawer."

Kip had no trouble with that, either. "You want some of this powder and lotion stuff?" he asked, studying the other containers in the drawer.

"Better bring some powder," she said. "I think that helps prevent diaper rash." Then… "Maybe not. Would you mind getting the book on the nightstand in my room?" she asked as, sopping wet diaper removed, she was using a wet wipe on the littlest bottom he'd ever seen. "Look up diaper rash?"

Kip would've liked a chance to glance more thoroughly around Leslie's room, but went straight for the medical book on top of a stack on Leslie's nightstand, turning to the index as he made his way back across the hall.

She had the clean diaper situated under Kayla, but hadn't closed it.

"It says here that diaper rash is skin irritation caused by a diaper that's on too tight, or that rubs, or is left on too long…"

Kip looked up from the book. "Damn, my first night and I've already screwed up. I'm sorry, Les."

"Would you stop?" she said softly. "She doesn't show signs of diaper rash yet. What do we do to prevent it?"

"Wash the area thoroughly."

"Done."

He read on. "It says to let her dry naturally before you cover her up again."

Leslie looked back at the child. "I think she's had time for that," she said after a moment.

Kip trusted her on that one.

"It also says to use an ointment with zinc oxide." He named the brand the book suggested. "Do we have any of that?"

Leslie nodded. "In the drawer. It comes in a white tube."

He found it. Removed the lid. And stared at the thick white toothpaste-like stuff.

"I think it's spoiled." Not only did it look questionable, it stank.

"It's not spoiled," Leslie took it from him. "I just bought it."

Didn't mean it wasn't spoiled, but Kip deferred to her greater knowledge. What he knew about babies was the few sentences he'd just read in her book. She'd had a whole week of this stuff.

Kip watched as she squeezed the ointment on to her fingers and then smeared it over the toddler's diaper area. And hoped that little Kayla didn't need this treatment often. It looked…uncomfortable.

Kayla turned her head and Kip held his breath, watching the tiny face for signs of waking. If she did wake, if she couldn't get back to sleep, he'd have to stay up with her.

The whole thing was his fault to begin with.

She turned her head again, eyes still closed, as Leslie secured the diaper with two easy swipes of pre-attached tape. That was all it took to put on a diaper?

He could do that.

CHAPTER NINE

"SO HOW WAS THE FIRST WEEK?"

Leslie, back in Juliet's office the following Friday, gave a little tug to the pale-pink turtleneck sweater she had on beneath her gray tweed suit.

"Fine," she said. And when Juliet gave her *that* look, added, "Good."

Only a few years older than Leslie, with long blond hair and a bohemian wardrobe, Juliet was the only human being Leslie had ever trusted completely. And there were still things she kept to herself. Important things...

The other woman smiled from the old armchair she'd bought for comfort, not style. "So what aren't you telling me?"

"You told me it's healthy to withhold certain...information. Of my own choosing. You said I should know I always have the right to private thoughts."

It was that right that had allowed her to come to Juliet in the beginning, to tell her about the past, without disclosing the one thing she'd never told another soul. And promised herself she never would.

"Uh, huh," Juliet said, her expression patient. Compassionate. Knowing. "So we're just going to sit here for an hour and look at each other?"

The woman saw too damn much. Which was part of the reason Leslie trusted her so much.

"My mother's due in next weekend. She's been working with a local Realtor. Kip and I went to look at a house for her in my community and she bought it last night."

"How do you feel about that?"

Leslie smiled. An easy question with an easy answer. "Really good."

"Why?"

"It'll be great to have help with the kids."

"Do you feel as though you're in the middle of the lake without a life preserver and you never learned to swim?"

"No."

Juliet nodded. And Leslie hated that. She always felt that nod meant she should be gaining some insight about herself.

"So, you're just holding on until your mother, with her greater experience and wisdom can save the day?"

"No."

Was she *supposed* to be doing that?

"I mean, we seem to have had more rough moments than easy ones this week, but that's to be expected, isn't it?" she asked. Or was she just barreling ahead, possibly hurting the kids in her inability to see that she needed guidance?

"What kind of rough moments?"

"Well…" She tried to come up with the worst, trusting Juliet not only to keep whatever she said confidential, but to let her know if she was making a mess of things without realizing it.

"One night at dinner, I'd made squash, which Jonathan hated, and Kip told him he had to eat it because it was good for him. Jonathan started to cry. Which upset Kayla. She began throwing all the food on her high chair tray."

Leslie paused at Juliet's humorous expression. "What?"

"Sounds like a typical family moment to me."

She hadn't gotten to the really horrible part yet. "I'd had a particularly nonstop day at the office and saw my house being trashed and Kip sitting there looking completely out of his element, and I just lost it," she confessed. "I hollered at Jonathan to knock it off, and grabbed Kayla's arm and wouldn't let her throw any more food."

"And what happened?"

"Jonathan stopped crying. Kayla put the food in her hand in to her mouth."

Juliet's expression grew pensive. Leslie waited, hardly daring to allow herself another thought until she heard the verdict.

"So, why else are you glad your mother's moving here?"

What? Where did that come from?

Still…if Juliet really wanted to know…

"The one thing I've hated about the past ten years is not seeing my mother much." She glanced around the room, at the flowers, the books, the magazines on a side table by the door, the ever-present water cooler. "I love my mother a lot," she said, looking straight at Juliet. "Not just because she's my mother, but because she's savvy and smart, and in her own way, emotionally strong."

Juliet sat silently, an invitation for Leslie to ramble.

"We never went through that stage where I felt sure I was smarter than she was and argued with everything she said and hated her control over me."

"Why do you think that was?"

She shrugged. She hadn't come here to talk about her mother. "I didn't have to fight for my freedom. She just gave it to me."

"I'll bet you thought you were the luckiest kid on earth."

"No, actually, I hated it," she said, surprised that Juliet was so far off. "Would've liked her protection."

"From what?"

Juliet knew from what—at least in part. It made her question disturbing. Leslie wasn't talking about that today.

"Life, the world, anything I didn't understand. I always had the feeling she expected me to figure things out for myself…."

Kind of like Juliet.

"Why did you need protection from life?"

"It's scary when you're a teenager," Leslie said, glancing at the clock on the wall one more time. "Listen, Juliet, there *was* a reason why I wanted to see you. Something I want to talk to you about…"

Leaning forward, Juliet clasped her hands over her knees. "What's that?"

"We've got this situation with Jonathan…."

Leslie described, as quickly as she could, what Kip had told her late the previous Friday.

"And has he changed or bathed Kayla since?" Juliet asked.

"Not yet. He hasn't needed to. I take her to day care with me and I've been off early enough all week to pick her up."

Juliet cocked her head, watching her. Leslie withstood the perusal with discomfort. She hated being analyzed.

"Do you have a problem with him doing those chores?"

"No! Of course not."

"But you understand Jonathan's point of view."

"I didn't say that."

"So you're saying you don't?"

"No." Leslie frowned. "I do."

"Why?"

"I'm good at that." The words gave her a curious kind of strength. "I have a talent for putting myself in others' shoes, seeing other perspectives." A statement that was okay within the sacred walls of Juliet's office, but not something she'd ever utter during any normal human interaction.

"So why get defensive when I first said that you understood?"

Leslie's mind went blank. And then replayed the last five minutes.

"It's okay, Leslie, you don't have to answer." Juliet's soft voice penetrated the haze.

Leslie nodded.

And when she appeared to be satisfied that she had Leslie's attention again, the counselor said, "Do you mind if I ask one more question?"

"Of course not."

"What do you think about the boy using your brother as a scapegoat for his own feelings?"

"Because Cal's not here to defend himself, you mean?"

"No," Juliet said, hands still in her lap. "I was referring to Jonathan's pawning his feelings off on his father rather than owning them himself."

Oh. "I…that's kind of normal, isn't it? For a kid to use his parent for support? I sure did when I was growing up and someone wanted me to go somewhere I knew I shouldn't. I'd say my mother said no even if I hadn't asked her."

Forearms now resting on her knees, Juliet met and held Leslie's gaze. "Do you believe your brother told his son that little boys—and apparently dads—don't look at naked little girls?"

Yes. "I have no idea."

Juliet stood. "You might want to think about it," she said, crossing over to her desk. "I'm assuming you're keeping your regularly scheduled appointment next week?"

"Yes." Leslie stood, too, not feeling a lot better. "If that's okay."

"Of course it's okay." Juliet grinned at her. "You're welcome here anytime, you know that."

It was still reassuring to hear.

"So what's going on with you and Kip?" Juliet asked as she walked Leslie to the door.

"Nothing, why?"

Juliet smiled at her again, the knowing smile that made her uncomfortable—usually defensive—and always made her think about whatever she'd said.

"No reason," her counselor said before wishing her a good day.

She might've had one if Juliet hadn't just ruined it for her.

The worst part was, she didn't even know how.

"Did you ask your counselor about Jonathan?"

It was late Friday night. The kids were asleep after an evening of running and screaming and laughing to their hearts' content at a local pizza establishment that specialized in a multitude of circus and video games and a colorful climbing apparatus for children under twelve.

After which, back at the house, he and Leslie had retreated, as had become their established practice, to their own sides of the house. They each had their own kid in tow, ready to supervise bathtime, story reading and, best of all, as far as Kip was concerned, lights out. His reaction was mostly one of relief—because bedtime meant he'd made it through another day without screwing up.

"Yes." Leslie sipped the glass of fresh-squeezed lemonade he'd poured. She'd declined the wine he'd offered.

"And?" He'd been waiting all day to hear about this. It was why he'd asked for this late-night meeting in the living room.

Well…partly. He'd started concocting reasons to spend time with his new housemate.

Not that he wanted her to know that. Not yet, in any case…

Leslie, still dressed in the suit she'd worn to work, slid down until her head was resting on the back of the sofa. She didn't seem to notice, as Kip did, that the more she moved one way, the more her skirt slid the other.

He wasn't complaining about having more thigh to enjoy. But he'd rather she was aware that he was enjoying it.

"And…" The answer had been too long in coming. "She really didn't have much to say."

"Did she recommend that we take him to see someone?"

"No."

"So she wasn't worried, then?" he asked, more relieved than he'd expected.

He was getting in deep with this father stuff.

"She just asked me a couple of questions about my feelings about it all," Leslie said, clearly exhausted—but relaxed, too? "It's what Juliet does when she wants me to come up with answers on my own."

"What kind of answer would you have about something like this?"

She looked at him, her eyes serious, although she gave him a small grin. "That's what I've been asking myself. And before *you* ask…" She held up her glass as though it were a stop sign. "No I haven't come up with anything."

Leslie sipped her drink, seemingly content to sit there, with him, in the softly lit night.

He liked watching her this way. Hell, he seemed to like watching her whether she was lounging on the couch with a sexy amount of thigh showing or wearing mashed potatoes on her eyebrows while yelling at tantrum- and food-throwing children.

Maybe he should pour himself a whiskey. Stiff enough to help him sleep alone.

"Didn't you say last night that you have a dinner meeting next Tuesday?"

"Yeah." She studied him from beneath her lids.

"I'll need to put her to bed then."

"I know."

"What do I do about Jonathan?"

"The only idea I can come up with is to distract him, don't let him know what you're doing, but that seems wrong to me."

"And fraught with damaging complications if he finds out."

"So what do you think?" she asked.

Uneasily Kip glanced at her. Then decided to get himself a lemonade. "I think you should talk to him," he said, dropping down on the opposite end of the couch when he returned with his glass of the beverage that was both sweet and tart.

Reminded Kip of the woman sitting so close to him. She turned her head. "Why me?"

She sounded more curious than defensive and he took heart. Okay, Leslie was more sweet than tart.

"Because you're a girl. You can explain it from a woman's perspective, tell him it's okay for fathers to take care of their little girls. He'd be more apt to believe it's true coming from one of 'them,' so to speak."

She nodded slowly.

"I'm sure his own mother would've handled this quite naturally from the time Kayla was born had she lived."

"Probably."

Kip took a small sip. "And you can tell him it's okay

for brothers to help, too," he continued, on a roll now that he was actually getting something right in the parenting department. "That way he won't feel—"

Leslie turned away, lifted her head. "No."

"Okay…" And then, when she appeared to have nothing further to add, he asked, "Why?"

"I don't think it's proper, that's why."

"But…" He frowned. Something was very wrong here. And that didn't make any sense. "Cal helped you all the time…"

"He helped me with my homework, Kip. He stayed home with me when our mother was showing property. He might have helped me pull off my boots on snowy days. I was nine years old when our father died and Cal took over. I was potty-trained by then."

Her tone was light, filled with enough caustic humor to make him smile. He didn't feel like smiling and had no idea why. The way she was avoiding his eye? The stiffness with which she held herself?

Or was he imagining the whole thing? God knew, he was totally out of his element here.

He was tired. She was tired. And Cal had been a model brother. Of those three things he was sure.

JONATHAN LAY IN BED on Saturday morning, waiting for Kip to get up so he could, too. He was kinda hungry. He wanted some of that cereal with colored things in it that Kip had told Aunt Leslie he wouldn't die from if she bought it.

'Course, pretty much any time Kip made Aunt Leslie laugh, she did what he said. Jonathan hoped that meant Aunt Leslie liked Uncle Kip. Nana said people had to like each other to live in the same house.

He looked around the room he had in this house. It wasn't blue like his mom had made his. And Aunt Leslie didn't put cool things on the walls. But still, it was better than a running-away place. Way better.

Turning over on to his back, he stared at the ceiling. It had funny swirls on it. He could pretend they were race cars or tornadoes. And he could pretend that, if he was really, really good, better than he'd been the other night when he'd cried about eating squash, they'd keep him here with Kayla for a long time. Really, he'd been crying because he missed his daddy but didn't want Kip to think he didn't like *him*. Maybe he could stay till he growed up enough to drive. Then, if he had to, he could drive away 'stead of run away.

He had to be good. And Kip had to make sure Aunt Leslie kept liking him and he had to keep liking Aunt Leslie, too, so they could stay here for a long enough time.

Seemed like a lot of big *ifs* to Jonathan. He just didn't know anything better.

'Cept running away. If he figured they wanted to get rid of him, he'd run away before they kicked Kayla out, too.

THERE WAS NO ROUTINE for Saturday. But then they'd only had one Saturday together—the day after Jonathan and Kip arrived.

Leslie liked routine.

"Jonathan, did you guys have a Christmas tree at your nana's last year?" she asked as they were all sitting at the table just after nine. She'd made scrambled eggs for Kayla and herself. The boys were having a slightly less healthy breakfast of sugared cereal.

But they'd shared her and Kayla's toast.

Chewing, the boy nodded. He'd appeared in shorts, a sweatshirt, socks and tennis shoes that morning. One day that week, he'd come down wearing jeans and a tank top. Every day he reminded her of a mini Kip.

"Did you help her decorate it?" she asked. Jonathan hadn't warmed up to her as Kayla had, but she sensed that he liked her.

He shook his head. "Nana didn't do it," he said when he'd swallowed what was in his mouth. "Daddy did."

Cal again. Leslie's stomach tightened and she put down her fork.

"Would you like to help me decorate mine?"

Dark eyes wide, he grinned. "Kip, too?"

Only then did she dare look across the table at the man she was growing too used to having around—despite the fact that she kept forgetting to check with him before rushing ahead with her plans. She'd been making decisions on her own for a long time now.

"Fine with me," he said, sending her a smile that settled her stomach but made other parts of her jump.

Sitting there in khaki shorts and a navy pullover with the long sleeves rolled up past his elbows, the man was too gorgeous for any woman's good.

Especially for a woman who'd been hooked on him since the age of twelve.

"Do you have one here?" Kip said, staring at her as though he could read her mind.

She cleared it immediately.

"No," she said, wiping her mouth with her napkin. Taking a sip of juice. "No, we'll have to go get one."

"A *real* tree?" Jonathan asked

Leslie glanced at Kip, congratulating herself on remembering to do so.

And then, when his smile made her tingle in some very private places, she decided that being inconsiderate was the more prudent choice for the future.

"I think a real tree's the only way to go," he said.

"Twee?" Kayla chirped. And burped.

Jonathan laughed.

And Leslie, meeting Kip's gaze, wondered how she'd ever thought coffee in bed with a good book was a great way to start her weekend.

She had no idea what she'd just gotten herself in to, but at least the day was planned.

She'd tackle the next hurdle when she had to.

Which she estimated, looking at Kayla's hair glued straight up with egg, would probably be in the next five seconds.

CHAPTER TEN

GUYS LIKE HIM didn't often buy Christmas trees—at least not in Kip's experience. But if they did, he figured they'd probably expect to go someplace where trees grew so they could cut one down. It seemed like a guy thing to do.

Leslie took them to a fenced tree lot decorated with colored lights and run by an older couple sitting at a table outside a mobile trailer, fifteen minutes from her house. Other than the temporary fencing and rows and stacks of trees, the place was nothing more than a parking lot on a corner.

"We're getting our tree here?" he asked, pulling his brand-new Ford Expedition up to the fence as she'd instructed.

"You see any pine tree forests in Phoenix, Webster?" she asked, grabbing the car door as she sent him a sassy grin. "In case you missed it, you've moved to the desert."

"Twee!" Kayla screamed from behind him. In his peripheral vision he could see her little lighted pink tennis shoes kicking back and forth with excitement.

She was belted into a car seat similar to the one Leslie had in the back of her black BMW.

"Can we get out?" Jonathan called from the third seat in the vehicle—the place he'd insisted on because he was the oldest.

"Yeah," Kip called back, watching the boy from the rearview mirror as he unhooked his safety belt and dove over the seat in front of him, barely missing his sister's head with his tennis shoe.

They were in for another active day....

"THAT'LL BE NINETY-SIX DOLLARS, sir," the sixtyish woman seated in a lawn chair behind the table told him, tallying up his bill on an ancient calculator and writing the receipt by hand.

He handed over a hundred-dollar bill. They'd had to have a Fraser so the needles wouldn't fall off too soon. And it had to be seven feet tall so it would fill the window alcove in the living room.

Kip smiled at the silver-haired woman as he pocketed his four dollars in change.

"Can I watch them cut the end, Kip?" Jonathan asked, out of breath as he dashed up beside him.

"Sure, sport. Then we're going to have to figure out how to get that monster in the SUV."

"We'll have to put the seat down, huh?" the little guy asked, half skipping to keep up as Kip strode over to the two brawny college students who'd helped them. They had the tree lying sideways on a couple of mounts, preparing to saw a fresh cut on the bottom.

"It'll preserve the tree a bit longer," Leslie had told him before walking Kayla over to look at the giant inflated Santa Claus at the far corner of the lot.

"Nope. Where will you sit then?" Kip asked, grinning down at the boy. He'd never seen Jonathan so unreservedly happy. Dared he hope the little guy was adjusting to him—that he'd be able to give Jonathan a relatively happy childhood in spite of all the tragedy that had befallen his young life? "We'll strap it to the luggage rack."

The larger of the two men, a tattooed blonde with an earring in his eyebrow, glanced up as they approached.

"You cut it yet?" Jonathan asked.

Blondie stared at Jonathan. And then up at Kip. "He belong to a friend of yours?"

"No," Kip said, still feeling good about how the day was progressing. Behind him he heard Kayla jabbering something that Leslie seemed able to decipher, but that he couldn't understand.

While the smaller guy, a dark-haired pimply-faced kid, continued to saw, the blonde looked at Jonathan again. In just the second it took for the curious stare to land, Jonathan shrank, lost whatever joy had consumed him. Gazing down at the ground, the child backed up a step.

"He's mine." Kip had made no conscious decision

to say the words. They just came. But he was damn glad they did. Putting his arm around the little boy, he pulled Jonathan forward.

"What do you think, son? Did he cut it straight enough to fit the stand?"

Jonathan looked at the tree—more, Kip sensed, because he'd told him to than because he felt any interest—and nodded.

"Then let's get this tree home," he said, hoisting all seven feet onto his shoulder and across his back.

"I'll grab this end," the tattooed blonde said quickly.

"No, thanks." Kip turned, caught Leslie's eye and headed toward the car. "My boy and I can get this just fine, can't we, Jonathan?"

"Yes." Jonathan's voice was barely audible.

"Twee!" Kayla screamed from Leslie's arms.

Kip hoped the little girl's joy was contagious and that her brother would become infected.

THE SWEATER WASN'T NEW. But it was black and red. The best he could come up with for festive. And he'd thrown the black jeans in with last night's load of his and Jonathan's clothes. More importantly, he'd remembered to get them out of the dryer before he'd gone to sleep so he could wear them unwrinkled tonight.

Kip brushed his teeth. Ran a comb over his hair and thought about cologne, but decided against it. Too much. Whatever was left from this morning's splash of aftershave would have to do. He didn't want Leslie to get skittish and start borrowing trouble again.

He scowled at himself in the mirror. "You have no idea what you want, bud," he muttered under his breath.

Still, she'd agreed to a late dinner with him— well, to ordering pizza instead of sharing the kids' macaroni and cheese—and waiting until after the kids were in bed so they could eat in peace and quiet for once. They were going to eat in the living room in front of the newly decorated tree. Another suggestion from him. But the wine had been her idea.

Flipping off the bathroom light, Kip wandered around his spacious bedroom. His things had finally arrived a couple of days before. Most of them were in storage, but it was good to have his own sheets and towels, his full assortment of clothes—and books— around him. He checked his watch.

Jonathan was brushing his teeth and putting on his pajamas. Usually took three minutes tops. He liked to give the little guy some privacy before story time, but he'd been in there at least fifteen minutes.

"Jonathan?" He crossed the hall outside his suite and rapped on Jonathan's closed bathroom door.

He heard something drop, but the boy didn't answer. Why was the door shut? Jonathan never shut the door. Unless he was going to the bathroom.

"Jonathan?"

Still no answer.

Kip had been killing time, waiting to read the next couple of pages of *Huckleberry Finn* to Jonathan while Leslie bathed and read to Kayla on the other side of the house.

"Jonathan." He hated to be stern, wanted Jonathan to like him, to trust him, but what if he was having trouble in there? He rattled the door handle, surprised when it opened immediately.

"Jonathan?" He sounded like a broken record. And then he saw the boy—standing on the toilet, leaning over to see himself in the bathroom mirror.

"Jonathan! What are you *doing?*"

Little snippets of red hair lay all over the counter, in the sink, on the floor, and on the boy's light cotton blue-and-white pajama top. Most disturbing was seeing the disposable razor Kip had thrown in the trash that morning in the five-year-old's hand.

"Give that to me right now."

Jonathan's hand lifted slowly, his dark eyes wide and frozen on Kip's face. Leaning forward, Kip grabbed the razor—probably more forcibly than he should have. And that was when he noticed his can of shaving cream on the back of the toilet tank.

"You have about two seconds to explain yourself, young man," he said, his face inches from Jonathan's as he stood before him at the edge of the toilet, ensuring that the boy didn't fall and hit his head on the marble counter.

"I was just cutting my hair…." The words were mumbled so softly Kip hardly heard them.

"Why?" He wasn't angry, though his voice sounded harsh, even to him. He didn't know what he was at the moment.

Jonathan's thin shoulders moved up and down in a pathetic shrug.

"If you wanted a haircut, all you had to do was ask. You realize that, don't you?"

The boy nodded.

"So why didn't you ask?"

"I don't know."

Well, Kip didn't know either. And he had no idea what to do next. If Kip had ever pulled anything like this, his father wouldn't have been around to notice.

He looked down at his hand—and felt a fresh flood of emotion at the sight of that razor. He had no idea where the scissors on the counter had come from.

Mental note: tell Leslie they had to put everything even remotely dangerous up too high for kids to reach.

"What's with the razor?" he asked.

"The scissors wouldn't get it all off." Jonathan was still mumbling, his chin lowered to his chest.

"You were going to shave your head."

"Uh-huh."

"Speak up, Jon."

His second "Uh-huh," wasn't noticeably louder.

"Jonathan, look at me."

Slowly the boy raised his head.

"Why?"

"It's red."

"Yeah." Kip had thought the boy was proud of having hair like his father's.

"I'm black."

"Yeah." And then, with horror spreading through him, Kip understood—and wanted to flatten tattooed Blondie. "And you're white, too, son."

Jonathan shook his head. "Only my hair."

Whatever had held Kip upright suddenly slackened, leaving him weak. He pulled the boy down from the toilet and sat with him there on his lap.

"Not just your hair," he said softly. "Half of you is white, son. It's only the color of your skin that's more black than white. And no matter what you do, how you change your looks, you aren't ever going to change that, do you understand?"

Staring down at the floor, the boy nodded.

"Far more important, though, is for you to understand that you don't *need* to change that," Kip continued, desperately searching for words. "You are part of two very intelligent, kind, giving people, young man. You have the best of both of them in you, and you have nothing to be ashamed of, you got that?"

The boy nodded again, but Kip knew his words hadn't done a thing for Jonathan's self-esteem. It could take years of solid love and positive example to do that—to combat the negatives, the curiosity and the rudeness—he would probably always face from some people.

Kip had no idea if he could be that solid, that positive. He just knew he had to try.

"Okay," he said, lifting the boy's head with a finger beneath his chin. "Now." He picked up the blue plastic razor from the counter where he'd dropped it. "You see these blades?"

Jonathan's head moved up and down against Jonathan's sweater, leaving stray little strands of red.

"Those are dangerous, and little boys aren't allowed to touch them. Ever."

Jonathan didn't respond—leaving Kip at a loss.

"They could hurt you badly."

Still nothing.

"We'll go and get your hair properly cut."

"'Kay," Jonathan whispered.

"And I have to punish you for taking that razor, Jonathan."

The boy stiffened, but stayed on his knee.

"What would be a good punishment?"

Jonathan pulled his head back, frowning at Kip. "What?"

"Kids don't say the punishments," he said slowly. "'Dults do."

Dammit, Kip thought, he couldn't do everything. Where was Leslie when he needed her? "Who says?"

"I dunno." The words were accompanied by one of Jonathan's frequent shrugs.

"Fine. If it's up to me, I say that we decide together what the punishment should be."

Ha! He'd sounded pretty damn good.

"Oh."

"So what do you say?"

"Going to bed without dinner?"

"You need your nutrition."

"No storytime."

"Reading's good for kids."

"A...spanking?" The little boy's voice wavered.

"I don't believe in corporal punishment."

"What's corporal punishment?"

"Hitting."

"Oh."

When they'd sat there so long Kip was afraid Leslie would eat by herself, it finally came to him.

"You have to sit and watch me shave every morning for a week," he said in the sternest voice he could find. "That way, you'll see how careful even I have to be when I touch razors. Got it?"

"But, Kip, I'm still sleep then."

"You'll have to get up half an hour earlier."

Jonathan glanced at him, his eyes serious. "Don't kids need sleep, too, just like n'trition?"

"Yep," Kip said, standing. "Which is why you're going to bed half an hour earlier every night for the next week."

At the slump of Jonathan's shoulders, Kip felt a little skip of victory. He'd meted out his first punishment and apparently it had hit its mark.

Think of it. Kip Webster a father.

The thought gave him shivers.

HE'D CHANGED HIS CLOTHES. She hadn't. Pulling the slightly damp white turtleneck with little colored Christmas lights splattered across it away from her body, Leslie savored the bite of meat-lovers pizza in her mouth. She rarely ordered pizza. And when she did, it was veggie.

At least they were both wearing jeans. Although she didn't know why any of it mattered. They were housemates eating pizza on Saturday night. It didn't matter that her heart jumped every time he moved. Or that she was feeling a bit like the schoolgirl with a crush she'd once been. Those days were long ago and far away. She'd had lots of moments in his company since then without those feelings.

Another bite of pizza helped seal the thought.

The present was what mattered, what was real.

She took a sip of wine.

They were just two people who happened to be raising a pair of orphaned siblings. Nothing more.

With that in mind, she filled him in on Kayla's latest—chomping on the bar of soap she'd insisted on holding, and then screaming at the top of her lungs when the taste of it hit her tongue.

"You want to hear the good part?" she asked, grinning at him over her wineglass.

"Of course."

"When her tongue started to burn, she reached out for me." She could still feel the thrill of it all the way to her toes. "She wrapped those independent little arms around my neck and held on the entire time I rinsed her mouth and then stood as quietly as an angel while I dried her."

Kip held up his wineglass, tipping it toward hers. "Congratulations."

Other than the dim table lamp she'd left on over by the hall, the colored lights from the Christmas tree were the room's only illumination. This had been a good idea of his—a quiet, peaceful dinner.

"Thank you," she said, touching her glass to his before taking a sip. She'd carried in paper plates, napkins and the wine. He'd set their places on the coffee table in front of the couch.

The only thing Leslie wished she'd changed was her wardrobe. She felt like leftover mashed potatoes sitting next to filet mignon.

"You seem quiet tonight." She regretted the words as soon as they came out. They were too intimate. Too personal.

That was what she got for relaxing, even for a second.

"I'm worried about Jonathan," Kip said.

"I noticed he wasn't as enthusiastic about the tree

after we got it home. I thought maybe he was missing his dad."

"Maybe," Kip agreed, but then told her about the rest of what had happened that day.

"Was the guy rude?" she asked, angrier than she'd been in a very long time.

"Not really," Kip said. "I almost wish he had been. I'd have had a reason to take him down a notch or two."

She frowned, a piece of pizza halfway to her mouth. "Is that what you want to teach Jonathan?" she asked. "To fight his way through people's ignorance and prejudice?"

Kip was sitting forward, his plate on the table. He wiped his hands on his napkin, swallowing. "I suppose not."

"We aren't going to be able to change the world, Kip," she said when he just sat there, neither eating nor drinking. "We can only give them enough love and security to face the world with their heads high. They're wonderful kids, smart, funny, independent, kind. *That's* what we have to show them. Then they can show the world. I know it's a cliché, but this is a case where I really think it's true that actions speak louder than words."

He glanced sideways at her, sending a silent message as he held her gaze. Saying thank you? Asking for help? She wasn't sure.

"This isn't going to be easy, is it?" he asked.

She reached for the red-and-gold-and-black crystals at her neck. "Not one minute of it, I'm afraid."

"I'm afraid, too."

If she'd lived to be a thousand, she would never have expected to hear those words from Kip Webster. People like Leslie lived life in fear. People like Kip lived it completely.

CHAPTER ELEVEN

LEFTOVER PIZZA SAT in plastic storage bags in the refrigerator. The box was out in the trash. But there was still wine in the bottle.

Kip carried it in to the living room where Leslie was sitting, empty glass in hand, staring at the Christmas tree. He filled her glass, and his own, before joining her on the couch.

"This is my favorite part of Christmas," she said, as unusually relaxed and mellow as she'd been all evening.

"Putting up the tree?"

She shook her head, red curls tumbling around her face and shoulders. He'd begun to spend a lot of time wondering what that hair felt like trailing through a man's fingers.

"No, sitting at the end of the day with a glass of wine, the quiet and the Christmas lights." She chuckled a bit self-consciously. "You're going to think I'm wacky, but I get more of a sense of hope from moments like that than any other."

He tried to find her wacky. It would be one hell of a lot easier. Instead, he was enchanted.

"Why?"

She looked back at the tree. "I don't know. The lights seem to suggest…possibility. And because it's a Christmas tree, the possibilities can only be good."

All he saw were branches with little lights casting a colored glow.

"Go ahead, you can laugh."

"No." He wanted to watch her, but kept his eyes on the tree. "It's nice. Your ornaments are all so different, you never run out of things to look at."

"I've collected them over the years," she said. "On my travels, or just when I'm out shopping. Anything that appeals to me I pick up."

"And the handmade ones?"

"I've done one or two, but mostly they came from charity bazaars."

The words brought to mind an instant picture of Leslie, with her cool façade, professional clothes and jewels walking around some charity bazaar. Probably in a church kitchen. Or maybe someone's home.

She'd be the type who wouldn't think about leaving without buying.

"What about you?" she asked. He could feel her looking at him. Tried to resist the urge to look back. And glanced over, anyway. Her eyes were in shadow, but the small smile tilting her lips was enough to send desire shooting through him. "Where are your ornaments?"

And then the smile faded as she set down her

glass. "I'm so sorry, Kip, I never even thought…" With one leg up on the couch between them, she leaned toward him. "I just brought down the boxes of my stuff without even asking if you wanted to use yours…."

"I don't have any."

"You didn't bring them, you mean?"

"I mean I don't have any."

"What happened to them?"

"Nothing."

She was staring at him, mouth open. Kip shrugged. "To tell you the truth, this is the first Christmas tree I've ever had."

"Since you were on your own, you mean."

"No." He shook his head. "I mean ever. You might remember that my father wasn't all that attentive."

"But you never came to our house at Christmas…what did you do all those years?"

"Lay around, watched TV."

"That's terrible!"

Kip grinned at the horror in her voice, and was also oddly touched. "It wasn't that bad, Les," he said. "Your mother always invited me over. I could've done the whole family Christmas thing if I'd wanted to."

"You would've felt like an outsider. That would've been worse than being alone."

So she was astute as well as intelligent and beautiful.

"It was just a day." He told her what he'd told himself during all those years of watching Christmas shows on television while he ate whatever meal the housekeeper of the hour had left for him. He used to pretend, at least in the early years, that he was on the show, not just watching it.

"You never had presents?"

"Yeah, I did," he said, not wanting to remember anymore. He liked what he had before him a lot more. "Usually something grand and extravagant— like the Camaro convertible—and there'd be a wad of money, too."

Not wrapped, though. And generally not on Christmas day.

"Your father should be shot." She was still leaning toward him, her warm blue eyes consuming him.

"He's dead." Kip reminded her, sipping wine. His throat was dry.

"The man didn't deserve to have a child."

He couldn't argue with her there.

"I'm not so sure I do, either." Jonathan could have killed himself with the razor that he'd thrown so casually in the trash. The little boy could have sliced a vein in his temple while Kip stood preening across the hall, giving a five-year-old "personal space" to get ready for bed.

"Just from being with you the past week, I can tell you that's utter nonsense," Leslie said. "You've made some mistakes, and so have I, but so does every single parent who ever lived."

If there were too many parents who left razors lying around, the world would no longer have to worry about a population explosion, he thought sardonically.

"I can *tell* you this," Leslie continued, her compassionate gaze warming him in ways it shouldn't. "But I know I'm not going to convince you of anything."

She might. She was pretty damned persuasive. If she'd been anyone else, anywhere else, he'd lean forward just the little bit it would take to press his lips to hers. If she was anyone else.

"Can I ask you a question?"

She had to be completely oblivious to the effect she was having on him. She wouldn't be sitting there so close, so relaxed, if she had any idea of the temptations he was fighting.

Or the heat in his blood.

"Of course," he said, taking another sip of wine.

"If you had to pick the one person in the world who truly knows you, who would it be?"

He'd expected something much harder than that. "Cal."

She nodded, as though she'd expected the answer.

"That's right. And he thought you were not only deserving of a child, he gave you *his* child."

She had a point. There wasn't much about him that Calhoun Sanderson hadn't known. The good, the bad, the women—his friend pretty much knew it all.

Leslie licked her lips and Kip had to restrain himself from offering to do it for her. The house was too intimate, in spite of its size. The room was too close, the lighting too dim. The wine was too good. The Christmas tree holding the promise of a real home and family that weren't his. The woman too sexy.

Maybe that was the problem. He needed a woman. Not Leslie Sanderson. Just a woman. It had been a while. And he wasn't used to depriving himself.

"Thank you," he said, although he'd meant to excuse himself. He reached out a hand, pushed a curl back from the corner of her eye. "You're right. No one knew me better than Cal and he wants me to raise his son. *Me.*"

She didn't pull away from his hand as he'd expected. As he'd deserved. She might even have leaned into it. Or he might have moved closer.

"I know it's made a huge difference to me in the past couple of weeks. Every time Kayla throws a fit and I freeze and can't think and feel a panic attack coming on, I remember that he wanted me to have her, and somehow the panic is averted."

He found another curl to smooth away. "I would never have guessed you were the kind of person who has panic attacks."

"I don't," she said quickly. And then, with a bit of a smirk, "At least, not anymore."

Her face was inches from his. Soft beneath his palm. Her eyes captivated him. "What would you have to panic about?" His voice sounded embarrassingly soft.

She licked her lips again. "Right now, I'm not aware of a thing," she told him.

He believed her. He wasn't aware of much himself. Except maybe her breasts, how incredibly tempting they were, pressing against the white cotton of her shirt.

"Kip?"

"Yeah?"

"Are you going to kiss me?"

"I'm thinking about it."

She nodded. Said nothing. With his thumb he gently touched the corner of her mouth. She let him.

"How about you?" He was impressed with his ability to form coherent words.

"What about me?" Her lips moved against the pad of his thumb.

"What are you thinking about?"

"Whether or not it'll be as good as I imagined back in junior high, when I had the crush of all crushes on you."

Kip was not a stupid man. No way in hell was he going to refuse that challenge. Still…

"You had a crush on me?"

"Don't pretend you didn't know."

He shook his head. He wished he had known, although he wasn't sure why. It wasn't like he would've done anything about it. Other than stay away from the Sanderson home.

So it was a good thing he hadn't known.

"You were always such a private little thing…."

With desire for her consuming him, Kip couldn't reason, couldn't even care that he couldn't reason. He moved slowly toward her until his lips finally touched hers.

He'd meant the kiss to be gentle—a simple *hello*. But as soon as he felt the sweet softness of Leslie's mouth, Kip could only react. Lifting her right off the couch, he settled her in his lap, turning her to brace her head against his arm. He nudged her chin with his and, as her mouth fell slightly open, slid his tongue inside. Her lips moved against his, participating. But not her tongue. It was almost as if she didn't know what to do with it.

Kip's desire swelled as he sought that tongue, coaxed it out to play, taught it how tease with his.

Then taking her bottom in his hands, Kip moved her against him, groaning with the delightful anguish—and then gasped for breath. He had to slow down. To savor this.

He didn't know how. Didn't recognize himself—or his reaction. Kip hadn't been an inexperienced schoolboy since his thirteenth birthday.

"You taste so good," he whispered against Leslie's lips. She groaned, reached for him again with lips that were wet and swollen. He pulled her tighter against him, feeling her breasts against his chest. She was woman everywhere. So much woman.

He couldn't get enough of her.

Her tongue eased lightly along his lips and he

loosened his hold on her, reaching between them to find the softness of her breast.

"Oh, God, Les, you feel good," he said, careful to touch tenderly, to please her. He found her nipple through her bra—it was hard and waiting for his touch. He teased her with the side of his thumb, then ran an index finger lightly around the tip. His mouth yearned to be where his hand was.

Sliding his hand beneath her shirt, he delighted in the satin of her skin against his palm, learning the contours of her stomach, her side. Her kisses, on the corner of his mouth, full on the mouth, inside— tongue touching tongue—were tentative and bold at the same time, innocent and hungry, dazing him with a desire that took away all conscious thought.

He found the front closure of her bra, fumbled as he slipped it loose and realized that his hands were shaking. The mound of her breast was womanly, both soft and full, enticing him to do things he'd never even considered doing to Leslie Sanderson. Her nipple was hard, and he rubbed his finger quickly back and forth against the tip, lifting his hips to her bottom as she groaned. He had to taste her. He had to—

"No."

"Huh?" He dropped her shirt, lifting his head as the quiet plea half registered. Or maybe it was just that she'd covered her breasts with her hands.

She didn't jump off his lap. Resting her forehead against his, she said, "I'm so sorry, Kip. I'm just—"

A rush of sweat, met by the room's air, cooled him enough to let him make his way through the fog.

"Don't apologize, Les, that was wonderful," he said, breathing heavily, meaning every word. He couldn't think of a time when kissing had been better.

"But I…"

"Ssh," he said, giving her a long, slow kiss. "You stopped a stupid man from rushing things for you." As soon as the ache in his body dissipated, he'd be grateful.

"You aren't mad?"

"Of course I'm not mad." Other than the ache that would pass, he felt great. Ready to laugh out loud with the unexpected and exhilarating turn of events. "It was our first kiss and I was taking us right on home. Insensitive of me, I admit."

She chuckled. "I suspect you often go right home on a first kiss."

Did she care about that? Did the other women bother her?

Kip laid his head back against the couch, watching her through lowered lids, bemused, confused. This ground was new to him—kissing a woman he was going to be seeing again every day for the foreseeable future. Kissing a woman he had history with.

"You aren't a woman to rush," he said when he sensed that she needed something from him.

"What does that mean?"

"Honestly?" He raised a brow, grinning at her.

She nodded, her lips swollen and gorgeous and so tempting.

"I don't know."

Leslie bowed her head, although the grin she was wearing relieved him. "It was good, wasn't it?" Her question was softly spoken.

"The best."

She glanced up. "Really?"

Holding her face between his palms, Kip looked her straight in the eye. "Really." He wanted to tell her how incredible, how different, holding her had been from any of the other women he'd held in recent years, but couldn't bring himself to be that vulnerable. So many changes in so little time—he needed time to catch up.

NERVES SINGING, Leslie sat next to Kip on the sofa, close but not touching, fear warring with a very timid and fragile hope as she experienced, for the first time, the aftermath of unrequited desire.

"So what do we do now?" She asked the question they'd both been avoiding for the past half hour. The wine bottle was empty, their glasses almost so. It was late. The kids would be up early.

"Go to bed?" he quipped, but while his mouth grinned, his forehead creased.

"Forget it ever happened?" she offered, half hoping he'd say yes. Maybe more than half hoping.

He glanced down at her. "Is that what you want?"

She could ask him the same question. And he could tell her that he'd asked her first. And they could play childish games and avoid the whole thing.

But they had to live together.

And she'd feel cheap. Bottom line for Leslie, she could not, would not, allow herself to feel cheap—like she had during that brief period in college. She might not find her way back a second time.

"No," she said now, slowly. "But I'm not sure what I do want."

"That's fair."

Peering up at him, she tried to chuckle like a woman of the world and managed a weak smile. "What does that *mean?*"

His eyes were warm, tender—he looked at her as though she were precious to him. Basking in that gaze, Leslie knew no fear.

"I think it's clear to both of us that we have to be very careful," Kip said, obviously choosing his words with care.

"We have the kids to consider," she agreed. "The most important thing is not to let anything that does or does not happen between us disrupt their lives."

"Parents fight, Les. Kids learn how to disagree in a healthy way by observing their parents."

She grinned for real and it felt good. "How would you know?"

"I told you I watched a lot of television."

"So it's okay if we fight? That's a relief." Inane

conversation, but how did you discuss sex with your housemate, who also happened to be the father of your child's sibling? Added to the fact that he was the one man in her life she'd ever had those feelings for…

Kip sighed and Leslie's heart opened up wide— too wide, she feared. "Listen," she said, taking his hand as she turned on the couch to face him. "The only promise we can make—*have* to make—is that we have honesty between us," she told him, knowing even as she said the words that they were going to burn her someday.

"I agree completely."

It was the response she'd needed. So why didn't she feel better?

She stared at the lights for a long time, sitting there holding his hand, saying nothing. She was tired, needed to sleep, and couldn't go to bed yet. She had to know…

"So…are we going to do it again?"

"Yes, I think we are."

She thought so, too.

And didn't see anywhere it could lead except to hell. Her own personal hell.

Unless she dared to hope.

MANY HOURS LATER, lying in bed alone, Leslie was still awake in spite of all her attempts to sleep, reliving the night, the incredible miracle she'd experienced, and its potentially tragic results.

Hand sliding to her breast, Leslie rested her palm there, gently, remembering the touch of Kip's fingers—and the shard of desire that shot down between her legs. Her other hand lay across her pelvis and tears dripped slowly down her cheeks.

That shard of desire was the miracle. She'd never once, in her entire life, known how it felt to *want* sex. To burn with physical need. She'd been craving that sensation her entire adult life, had feared that she'd die not ever knowing how it felt. The feeling was heady, stronger than self. There was no way on earth she could turn her back on it.

And that was the tragedy.

Because if things progressed, panic would soon replace anything that resembled a miracle.

CHAPTER TWELVE

SUNDAY AFTERNOON, while Kayla was down for her nap, Kip asked Leslie if she'd keep an eye on Jonathan for a while. He'd taken the boy for a haircut earlier that morning and Jonathan was still a bit subdued over the whole episode. But with the switchover at SI, Kip had some changes to make at the main facility—a couple of offices that needed to be cleaned out, others moved—and he'd prefer to get the work done while the hundred-member staff wasn't there.

Happy to spend some time with Jonathan, she'd also been glad of the respite from Kip's alluring company. All through breakfast, she'd been watching him—and vacillating between anticipation of a future she'd only dared hope for on the periphery of her mind, and a heaviness she knew well.

Earlier, she'd set Kayla up in her suite in front of a Disney video with a box of crayons and an oversize pad of white paper. Sitting on the floor with her, Leslie had perused the journals she'd kept during her years of intense therapy with Juliet. In those long months, she'd discovered, very slowly, that she was worthy, she was competent, she was beautiful and talented and had much to contribute to the world.

"Cwy?" Kayla's baby voice had brought her out of her deep reverie to see the child staring up at her, pink overalls giving her cheeks a rosy glow.

"Nana cwy?"

"I'm Aunt Leslie," she said, rapidly wiping away tears she hadn't noticed. Then she touched the little girl's cheek with the back of her knuckles. "But you can call me Mama if you'd like."

Kayla's brows drew together, as though she was considering the offer.

"Nana cwy?"

"No, Aunt Leslie isn't crying anymore," she said, chuckling as she lifted the child onto her lap, uncaring about the wrinkles that would leave in her navy cotton slacks, pulling the pad of paper and crayons with her. "Now, let's see if we can get some more color onto this page...."

While they'd been sitting there, Kayla had only used one crayon—brown. Leslie understood the choice. There were times in life when keeping things basic just felt safe.

LESLIE FOUND JONATHAN in the living room, running a plastic train engine around the Christmas tree when she came in from putting Kayla to bed. Kip had left about five minutes before.

The boy, with his very short haircut, was wearing

navy-and-white nylon sweatpants, a navy T-shirt and white tennis shoes today. Leslie had begun to look forward to Kip's daily ensembles for his new son. If nothing else, Jonathan Sanderson was going to be the best dressed kid in his kindergarten class when school started again in January.

"What do you want to do this afternoon?" she asked, sitting on the edge of the couch.

Jonathan chugged and scooted. "I dunno."

She clasped her hands together, surprised by their sudden clamminess, and barely resisted wiping them along the arms of her long-sleeved white shirt. This was her first time alone with the boy, but he *was* just five years old. A child. Her brother's child.

"What would you be doing back in Ohio?"

Chugga, chugga, chugga. "I dunno."

"Do you want to read a book?"

The little boy sat back on his heels and looked at her. "I ain't good at it yet."

"You're not good at it."

Chin jutting out, he nodded.

"I could help you. Or read to you."

"Okay." He didn't sound all that enthusiastic.

"Is there something you'd rather do?"

"I dunno."

The afternoon was not going to be the respite she'd been hoping for. Wondering what mothers normally did to occupy their small sons, Leslie landed on the only thing she could remember her mother doing with her and Cal on any kind of regular basis.

"Let's make some cookies."

"HERE." LESLIE PUSHED the big silver mixing bowl across the island to rest in front of Jonathan, who was sitting opposite her on a bar stool. She held out a metal cylinder with a turning crank. "This is a sifter," she said. "Just turn that crank, and the flour and soda and salt will fall through the screen into the bowl."

The little boy frowned. Took the sifter. And turned it with jerky movements.

"Boys don't make cookies," he said so softly Leslie wasn't sure if she'd been meant to hear.

"Of course they do," she answered anyway. Dropping the unwrapped stick of butter in a pan, she added four squares of unsweetened chocolate. "Your daddy cooked all the time. *And* he baked."

At least he had when she'd known him. And since, as far as she was aware, he'd lived alone all of his adult life, she assumed he'd continued to do so.

"Not cookies," Jonathan said. "Only Nana made cookies."

"And you didn't help her?" She glanced from the pan on the stove, where the butter and chocolate were melting together with a cup of sugar, over her shoulder to see Jonathan shaking his head. And still cranking. Flour surrounded him on the beige-and-brown granite counter top. And spotted his cheek.

"Why not?" She wanted so badly to understand this child. To be close to him. She already loved him so much. And she feared some of the things he represented.

"Boys don't make cookies," he said again.

Leslie chuckled, more for Jonathan's sake than because her amusement was real. "Who told you that?"

"No one," he said, shrugging.

"So why do you say it?"

He turned harder, his tongue darting in and out of his mouth, the sifter resting against his navy T-shirt. It also was streaked with white.

"Never seen 'em."

She stirred slowly, checking that the heat was on low. "How often do you watch cookies get made?"

"Don't."

"But you eat them."

The kid grinned. "Yeah!" he said, his voice raising in glee.

"So, you know they get made because you eat them, but you really don't have any idea who makes them."

"Girls do."

"Have you *seen* all the cookies you eat get made by girls?"

"No."

"Then you can't prove they weren't made by boys."

"Can't be. Boys are playing ball," Jonathan said, setting the almost empty sifter on the counter.

"Finish that up, mister," Leslie said.

Jonathan started cranking again.

"And boys do a lot more than play ball," she added.

"Yeah, they work."

"And they watch television and they cook and they clean and they shop...."

Dropping the empty sifter on its side, Jonathan heaved a big sigh, shaking his head, which rested on the hand supported by his elbow. "You don't know much 'bout boys, huh?" he asked her.

"I know some."

The little boy jumped down from the bar stool, coming over to stand on tip toe beside her, peering into the pan.

"But not that boys don't make cookies," he muttered.

He was certainly persistent. Had Cal been just as stubborn? She couldn't remember.

Of course, she'd only been two when Cal was Jonathan's age.

"Boys do make cookies," she said, thanks to the years of therapy that had taught her to speak up when she had something to say. "*You're* making them and you're a boy."

Jonathan lost his balance, used a hand on her arm to steady himself. He didn't respond to her latest comeback, leaving her to wonder if she'd convinced him or if he'd just given up convincing her.

Or maybe the process of chocolate melting had distracted him. He was still watching the pan.

"As soon as this melts, we're going to pour the flour in here and then put the whole thing in the refrigerator until Kayla wakes up," she told him.

"You can't eat cookies out of a pan."

"And that's why, when your sister wakes up, we're going to make little balls out of the dough. We'll roll them in powdered sugar and then bake them."

He dropped down from his toes, wandering over to slump at the table. "When do we eat 'em?" He was clearly disappointed.

"As soon as they cool."

"Before dinner?"

One look at his crestfallen face and her "absolutely not, young man" became "Yep." No question, she still had some parenting skills to learn.

An hour later, Leslie was just getting to the part where Huck picks up Jim, with Jonathan snuggled next to her, mouth open as he listened, when she heard Kayla jabbering upstairs.

"Come on, young man, your sister's awake," she said, giving Jonathan a squeeze.

He pulled abruptly away, as though only now realizing how close he'd been. The little guy was starved for physical affection yet didn't seem able to avail himself of it.

It was a predicament she understood. And she was scared to death to see it in her nephew.

"Let's go tell her hello and get her changed so we can make those cookies," she said lightly, while her heart beat heavily in her chest. She'd made Kip a promise and the moment had presented itself.

Get off the couch, Jonathan. Come upstairs with me. Be healthy and unaware—an innocent five-year-old boy.

"Can't," Jonathan said, arms crossed as he held his seat and stared up at her.

"What do you mean you can't?" she asked, grinning at him, thankful that she'd become so adept at pretending nonchalance, calm, ease, while hiding the panic inside her. "Are your legs broken? I didn't notice anything happening to them on the way in from the kitchen."

Jonathan frowned at her. "Boys don't be around naked girls."

"Boys don't stare at naked girls," she said. "And they don't ask them to get naked. But as long as boys are only helping take care of them when they're too little to take care of themselves, it's okay to be around."

She'd thought about what she'd say. Had come up with nothing. In the end, the words were just there.

"Daddy said no," the boy said, not budging an inch from his position on the couch. "And he said girls ain't s'posed to see naked boys, neither."

"I'm sure your dad had a good reason at the time." Leslie reached down, slid her hand beneath Jonathan's arm to find his hand and gently pulled. "But whatever it was, it's got nothing to do with right now. Come on, I need your help."

"Uh-uh." Jonathan shook his head adamantly, but sounded like he might cry.

Torn between the baby chatter coming from down the hall and the struggling boy, Leslie sat down on the couch again. Kayla knew how to turn around backward and slide off the end of her bed. And there was nothing in her room that could hurt her.

"Hey, Jonathan?" She waited until his dark eyes were trained on her face. "Remember how you told us about Easter time and your daddy gave you that chocolate bunny and you ate the whole thing all at once and it made you sick?"

He nodded, looking guilty.

"Did that mean the chocolate bunny was bad?"

Mouth open again, he shook his head.

"It just meant that the way you chose to *use* it was bad, huh?"

He nodded.

"Nana!" came from down the hall. Apparently the toddler had decided to remain in her bed until she was collected.

Judging by the tone of the last call, Leslie might be running out of time.

"And what about when you and Kip were wrestling on the floor the other night," she said, trying to ignore the shaking in her hands. "That was fun, huh?"

The little boy nodded. He wasn't saying much, but at least she had his attention.

"What if you'd really been fighting and someone had gotten hurt?"

Jonathan shrugged. "I dunno."

"Sure you do," she said, nudging his chin as she smiled at him. "It wouldn't have been fun," she told him. "In fact, it would've turned something fun into something bad."

He nodded again.

"It's that way with almost everything, honey," she told him, afraid she was failing completely here, all the while sensing how vital this conversation was to her nephew's emotional health. "There's a good way and a bad way to do things. Just like with the chocolate bunny—instead of enjoying it a bit at a time, you ate it all at once and made yourself sick. Does that mean you should never have a chocolate bunny again?"

"No."

"No, it doesn't."

"Cwy!" Kayla's wobbly voice wasn't lacking in volume despite its distress.

"It's the same when you're taking care of people," she told him. "Both boys and girls. Kids need help. That's the way God made them. And people are supposed to help them. Now, does everyone do the right things—make right choices?"

"No."

"Some people might ignore a kid who should be helped. Other people might hurt them, instead. But does that mean we should all quit helping?"

"No."

"No, it doesn't." She sounded like a broken record. Jonathan was watching her, his face impassive. Was she making a difference? Was she reaching him at all?

Or, God forbid, was she making things worse?

"Your nana helped you." Jonathan didn't budge.

"What if you and Kayla and I were here alone overnight and you were taking a bath and fell and hit your head?"

His eyes grew wide, but he said nothing.

"I'm a girl. Should I just stay away and let you bleed to death?"

"No!"

"Of course not," she quickly assured him. "Don't you see, honey? If that happened, it wouldn't matter that you were naked. I wouldn't pay any attention to that. I'd just help you."

Jonathan nodded one more time.

"And it's the same with Kayla," she told him, braced to have him close himself off again. "Sometimes Kip and you will be here alone with her, and she's going to need help with certain things because she's too little to take care of them herself."

His hand remained in hers. Leslie took a deep breath and plunged ahead.

"As long as all you're doing is helping her, and you aren't misusing that privilege by looking at things you don't need to look at or touching places you don't need to touch—like you misused the privilege of being given a whole chocolate bunny by eating it all at once—then you're being a very good boy. Not a bad one."

He remained silent. Staring at her.

"Okay?"

"I dunno."

"NANANA! CWY!" The baby had worked herself up to a full scream.

"Come on." Leslie took a chance. "Kayla needs our help."

Slowly, watching her with obvious doubt in his eyes, Jonathan slid off the couch and walked down the hall beside her.

"Hɪ, Mᴏᴍ." Leslie held the phone to her ear with both hands, sweating and shaking so much she was afraid she might drop it.

"Hi, honey! Just five more days until moving day!"

Clara was flying out the following Saturday night, after supervising the movers as they loaded her possessions on the truck.

"I know," Leslie said. "I can hardly wait. I had no idea raising kids was so exhausting."

Clara chuckled. "I'll be there soon enough, sweetie, and eager to help wherever you need me."

Ironic that the timing was so off. If Clara had been as available eighteen years before…

Clara asked about the kids, how they were eating,

wanting to hear everything they'd said or done since she'd last talked to Leslie two days before. And she talked about Cal, sobbing a little as she told Leslie about an old yearbook she'd found under the bed that Cal had used growing up.

"How's Kip doing?" she asked about half an hour into the conversation.

"Good!" Leslie said, a whole other set of nerves giving her voice a little more energy than necessary. For some reason, recalling the kisses she'd shared with Kip the night before, while talking to her mother, brought, not embarrassment or humor but a huge sense of shame.

She'd worked through all that. Years ago. She had nothing to be ashamed of. None of what had happened when she was younger had been her fault. She had to believe that. *Did* believe that.

"Is he there now? I'd like to say hello to him."

"No," Leslie said quickly, pacing her bedroom, studying the grains in the wood floor as she held the mobile phone to her ear. "He's been gone since early this afternoon—moving things around at the office. The buyout becomes official tomorrow, and there were a few disgruntled people who opted for early retirement. He wanted them out before they had a chance to poison any of the other staff."

"He's a good man."

"Yes, he is."

"Nice-looking, too."

Leslie stared out the window into the darkness of the mountain behind her house. Had the whole world gone mad?

"Yes, he is."

"It must be kind of strange, having a man living there with you after you've been alone for so long."

"It is, a little," she said, her stomach so tightly knotted it hurt. She couldn't have this conversation with her mother. "But not as hard as you'd expect. This is a big place. He has his suite and I have mine, each with our respective kid across the hall. It's not very different from living next door to each other in two separate apartments." Leslie didn't often lie, but the words fell smoothly off her tongue.

"Oh." Was that disappointment she heard in her mother's voice? Clara had given up nagging her about her love life years ago, after Leslie had uncharacteristically run out of patience during a phone call. Clara had been worried about Leslie isolating herself too much, and Leslie had lost her temper. They'd recovered from that episode mostly by pretending it had never happened, but after that, Clara didn't ask about male companions.

"We put up the tree yesterday," Leslie said now, infusing her voice with a cheer she didn't feel. "Did you know that Kip's dad never got a tree?"

"I didn't," Clara said. "But I wondered. I practically begged Kip to come and spend the holiday with us. Even called his father once to try to make some arrangements, but neither one of them ever took me up on it."

"Well, he'll be having it with us this year," she said, in an attempt to make up for any letdown she might have caused her mother a few minutes before. And for the same reason, she remained on the phone, chatting about presents and menus and the going-away party the McCulloughs had thrown for her mom the night before, for another twenty minutes when all she wanted to do was crawl beneath her covers and cry herself to sleep.

CHAPTER THIRTEEN

KIP ARRIVED HOME much later than he'd expected. He'd always been used to returning to an empty place, with only the timed lights on to greet him, and yet he was a bit shocked by the disappointment that swept through him when he came in to find that everyone had already gone to bed.

He'd figured the kids would be asleep. But he'd been hoping Leslie would wait up for him.

Especially after the previous night.

Apparently those kisses hadn't meant as much to her as they had to him. The memory had been distracting him all day. As had fantasies of repeating them that evening.

He thought about having a beer. Opened the refrigerator door. Shut it again. He didn't want a beer. The scent of fresh-baked cookies wafted from the jar on the counter. Chocolate pixies she'd called them. Said he'd like them. Maybe tomorrow.

Tonight he wanted conversation. He wanted the fact that he was home to matter.

He was tired, he told himself, and needed to get a

grip. If he was going to have these kinds of expectations after only one kiss, she'd probably kick him out on his ass. And he wouldn't blame her a bit.

Of course, had she been the one out late, he would've waited up....

Stop it, Webster.

Kip wandered through the "communal" parts of the house, checking to make sure the doors were locked when he knew damn well they would be. Leslie kept her doors locked even in the middle of the day when she was home. And she'd remembered to turn off the lights, too.

She'd been living alone for more than ten years. She didn't need him to check the house for her.

About to turn around and head to his room, a shower and some sleep, Kip noticed light coming from beneath Leslie's door. *Had* she waited up?

Mood brightening, Kip walked quickly down the hall. Had she fallen asleep with the light on? Should he knock and find out?

Would she mind if he just told her he was home and had come to say good-night? That was the polite thing to do. He'd want her to come and tell him, if their situations were reversed.

And he couldn't have her thinking that last night had meant nothing to him. They were at least close friends now. Which merited saying good-night, didn't it?

He knocked softly, calm inside and out. And then

again, a little louder, conscious of Kayla sleeping across the hall.

Leslie still didn't reply. And he didn't want to knock any harder, didn't want to risk waking Kayla.

He stared at the doorknob, considered turning away and going to bed. But he didn't want to do that at all.

Should he just walk right in? It would be an infringement of her privacy. They couldn't go around doing that—not and share a house with any measure of comfort or ease.

But what if she'd fallen asleep with the light on? *Nice try, but she can afford the bill, idiot.*

So…what if she was sick? Or hurt? He'd only been living with her a matter of days, but he already knew that Leslie wasted nothing. Including electricity.

That decided it. Turning the knob slowly, giving her a chance to call out, tell him no, he opened her door.

KIP'S FIRST INSTINCT, after wanting to crawl into bed and spoon with Leslie, was to quietly back out of her room. The light was a night-light, of all things. A purple glass angel outlined in metal, with a heart hanging down from a chain. It was plugged into a receptacle so far above her bed she must've had the outlet specially installed.

She was lying on her side, back to the door. Asleep, he assumed.

Until he noticed the pillow covering her head, the fingers clutching it. Or was it the slight shaking that first caught his attention?

"Les?" He didn't want to startle her—impossible considering the fact that he was in her room at eleven o'clock on a Sunday night and she was in the bed, expecting to be alone until Monday.

He knew he was trespassing, yet he couldn't go away and leave her. He knew he should. Was well aware that decency dictated it.

"Les?" he said a little more loudly, certain it would be less intrusive to get her attention that way rather than crossing over and taking her in his arms, which was what he longed to do.

She froze, the fingers on the pillow stiffening. All movement of her back and shoulders ceased. He couldn't even tell if she was breathing.

She'd heard him.

"I know I'm a complete jerk, standing here like this," he said. "I just came by to tell you I'm home and that I locked the door behind me…." He was rambling; he didn't recognize the pleading voice as his own. "I saw your light on and knocked and you didn't answer and…"

Still no movement. Her comforter, white with primary-colored squares, was pulled up to her ears. Her curls, wild and lovely, were spread around her. Wearing the jeans and sweatshirt he'd had on all day, Kip felt dirty.

"Just tell me you're okay and I'll go…."

Two words. *I'm fine*. That was all she had to say to get rid of him. The white and purple room was completely silent. No response.

"Les?" he said again, moving closer. "You're scaring me now."

Still nothing.

"Are you sick?"

He was beside the bed, looking over the mound of covers and pillows, searching for any glimpse of the woman beneath.

"Leslie." The word was a command to respond to him.

She didn't.

To hell with decorum, circumspect behavior, privacy. Kip grabbed the pillow, tugged it away from her and moved back a step as she released it. Her hands fell to the covers, as in capitulation.

What the hell was going on? The pillow dropped to the floor.

"Leslie?" Could he sit on the bed beside her? "Talk to me."

He sat. Brushed hair away from her face. The strands were soaked. So were her cheeks.

"Leslie?" His voice gentled while his heart raced. Touching her shoulder, he turned her carefully toward him, again with no resistance. He watched intently, expecting her eyes to be shut tightly against him. They weren't. Her lids were wide open, swollen. Did she even know he was there?

"Can you see me?" he asked, wondering if he should call 911—and what he'd tell them.

"Yes."

"Are you okay?"

She didn't answer. Just stared at him, as though waiting for something.

"You've been crying."

She nodded, her chin puckering as though she might start again. But in the next moment she'd calmed herself.

"I'm sorry for intruding. I was worried about you."

She nodded. That was all. No explanation. No recrimination. Nothing.

It was the weirdest situation he'd ever experienced.

Should he go? Was she going to be all right now?

"Why were you crying?" he asked.

She shrugged. "My way of coping, I guess."

Coping with what? He'd called several times that day. She and the kids had baked cookies. Had lasagna for dinner. Watched videos. Read books. Jonathan had helped her get Kayla ready for bed.

Miracle of miracles.

"Thank you for your help with Jonathan."

A shudder was her only response and Kip's heart quickened again.

"Did he give you trouble?"

"No."

What was she coping with?

"Do you want me to go?" He asked, afraid of her answer. "Move out, I mean?"

"No." There'd been no inflection in the answer.

"You sure?"

"Yes." No hesitation, either.

Kip's shoulders began to relax.

"Can you talk to me, then? Tell me what this is about?"

"No."

Okay, well, that was pretty definite.

"Is it something I've done?"

He had no idea what she had on beneath the covers. All he could see was white lace at her neck. Her arms were bare.

She continued to stare at him. "No."

"Something I'm not doing?"

"No."

He wracked his brain. "Has someone hurt you? Someone call today? Bad news at work?"

"No."

Her gaze was clear, her answers concise. She wasn't going to talk to him. He had to accept that.

"Okay, then, I'll see you in the morning."

She blinked. Looked kind of surprised. And then nodded.

"In the meantime, if there's anything I can do, just holler."

He turned, exhausted, with no idea of what had actually happened.

"Kip?"

Swinging around, he sought her eyes. "Yeah?"

"Can I, um, have a kiss good night?"

"Yes." Oh God, yes. Restraining himself from rushing back, Kip moved slowly, watching her the whole time, doing his best to silently communicate that she could trust him. No matter what was bothering her.

She reached up when he got to the side of the bed, pulling him down to her, eyes closed as her lips touched his. Kip followed her, letting her lead them wherever she needed to go. Passion held in check as he kissed her, thinking of her rather than drowning in the sensation she was evoking, Kip sat down, holding her close. His tongue danced with hers, his arms encircling her.

And when she dropped her arms, letting him go, he let go, too.

"Thank you," she said, her face unlined, almost peaceful-looking.

"You're welcome."

"Good night." She slid under the covers again.

"Night. Sleep well."

"You, too." The last was said with a sleepy sigh.

Kip tried. Far into the night he tried to sleep. But all he could do was replay that brief time in Leslie's room.

It was the oddest thing he'd ever lived through.

"HE TRIED TO make love to me on the couch again last night." Dressed in a forest-green suit with her gold-trimmed silk blouse beneath it, Leslie sat in Juliet's office the following Friday. She was there officially.

She'd called Juliet on Monday, telling her counselor she needed to be back in session, not just chatting. Juliet had responded with an immediate invitation to meet over the lunch hour. Leslie had opted for Friday's already scheduled appointment. She needed to know she could make it that long— that she was healed enough to cope with everyday life, even if she needed occasional help with demons in the night.

Juliet had called her midweek to check up on her, and Leslie had told her about Jonathan then. She'd saved Kip for today. Their hour was three-quarters gone, but she wasn't feeling much better.

"And?"

"Come on, Juliet," she said, jumping up to pace around the couch. "Haven't I been coming here long enough, haven't we shared enough, for you to just *talk* to me for once? React? Validate that because I was sexually abused and for the first time in my life feel sexual desire, there might be some trauma involved in carrying desire into reality? What's with this 'and' stuff—as though I'd just told you I was stopping at the bakery on my way back to work?"

Juliet's smile trembled a bit. A first, as far as Leslie could recall. "You're really okay, you know?"

It wasn't what Leslie had been expecting.

"What do you mean I'm okay? I'm not okay at all! Talking to a five-year-old boy about changing his little sister unhinged me. I panicked. Lay in bed thinking I was going to have a heart attack. Cried and didn't even know I was crying until I noticed the sheet was wet. That's *not* okay."

She turned, facing her counselor, so angry she couldn't get the words out fast enough. The tears in her eyes were angry tears, not interfering with her voice in the slightest.

Juliet's eyes held compassion. Understanding. Love. "I'm definitely not okay," Leslie said, depleted all of a sudden.

"Yes," Juliet said, nodding. "You are. You're fighting back, Leslie." She sounded so calm, so sure, that Leslie couldn't help listening to her. Considering the truth of her words.

"Rather than being a victim, you're angry and expressing your anger. You're admitting that you were abused as simply a fact, not as something to be ashamed of. You're demanding your rights, stating your needs."

"I'm scared to death." She was crying fully now, the pain inside her making it impossible to stop.

"I know," Juliet said. "But you're also healthy. You can do this, Leslie."

She glanced at the one person in the world she dared to trust. "It doesn't feel that way." A tiny lighted Christmas tree twinkled from a round table across the room.

"If it felt that way it would be easy. Life isn't meant to be easy. It's a series of challenges that we can either choose to conquer or be defeated by."

She'd made the choice to conquer ten years ago, when she'd been unable to find a single suit that would fit her size-zero body for her first professional interview. That was when she'd made an appointment to see Juliet.

"You've overcome anorexia, an addiction to over-the-counter sleep aids and a host of other self-defeating behaviors."

"I'm still afraid to sleep in the dark." She hadn't told Juliet about Kip's visit to her room on Sunday night. The memory was still too confusing, too private—and somewhat too precious—for analyzing. But she worried what Kip thought of a thirty-year-old woman who slept with a night-light.

"But you're getting past your isolation," Juliet said. "Look at you. Two months ago, you would never have had a dinner guest in your home. Today you have a family living there. *Your* family."

It was a miracle. And the source of her greatest fear.

"The panic attacks are back."

"Give yourself a break, woman!" Juliet leaned forward as Leslie sank back on to the couch. "You just lost your only sibling and you're making incredibly huge changes in your life. Anyone would panic a bit at that. Change, no matter how small or how great, brings about fear. It's natural."

"Do you think I should try to sleep without the night-light?"

"No." Juliet sat back. "One major challenge at a time, okay?"

Leslie smiled, as she knew she'd been meant to. "Okay."

"So…tell me about last night."

Leslie glanced at her watch instead. The hour was up. Touching the green, blue and gold crystals at her neck, she stood. "Time's gone."

"Sit!"

Leslie sat.

"Tell me what happened."

She didn't want to think about it.

"You going to come this far and then quit on yourself?" Juliet asked.

"No."

"I didn't think so."

"He'd been telling me about a major new account he'd closed for SI yesterday—a professional sports league. He was so humble about it, and so proud of himself at the same time, and without thinking I leaned over and kissed him. It kind of went on from there and…and I was feeling good," she said, not the least embarrassed with Juliet. The woman knew things about Leslie that no one else knew. Horrible things. Shameful things. Tainted things.

And while there was one important part she didn't know, she knew enough for her acceptance to contribute toward Leslie's healing—her acceptance of herself.

"…and then…when he undid my bra…touched my breast…"

"You panicked."

"Yes."

"What about the desire?"

"It was gone."

"Completely?"

"Mostly."

"But not completely?"

"I guess not."

She wasn't sure why it mattered, but now that Juliet had pointed it out to her, she was glad to know.

"The first time you were touched, you were twelve. Right?"

"Yes."

"And this man who touched you, someone you knew, he touched your breast?"

She was sweating. And cold. Sick to her stomach. Scared to death. "Yes."

"Which is why, when Kip touches you there, you shut down."

"I've been touched there hundreds of times since," Leslie said, the first derogatory comment she'd made about herself—out loud, in front of Juliet—in many months.

"You're referring to your promiscuous period during college."

Leslie nodded.

"You understand why you behaved that way and have already forgiven yourself for it."

She was right. Of course. Breathing easier, Leslie reached for a tissue. Sat back. Wiped her eyes and nose.

"Don't you have someone waiting?" she asked Juliet.

"My twelve-thirty cancelled."

So that didn't let her off the hook.

"If I don't make love with him, he's going to lose interest."

"Possibly."

"The only way I know how to make love is like I did in college."

"That wasn't lovemaking."

"I know. And I don't want that with Kip."

"You don't want that for yourself, ever again. You deserve to be loved. To love yourself. To love what you're doing. To enjoy it."

She started to cry. "What if I can't?"

"Was that a negative statement?"

"No," Leslie said, since such a thing was taboo during Juliet's sessions. And then, head high, "Yes."

"You'll never succeed with a defeatist attitude, Leslie."

"I know."

"There are no guarantees in life, ever. Not about

waking in the morning, getting home safely at night or anything in between."

In other words, worrying about what might or might not happen in the future was a waste of time. Borrowing trouble from the future, Kip would say.

She'd promised him she wouldn't do that.

Add it to the list of promises she'd made herself over the years and still struggled to keep.

"You know what to do."

She did. She just wasn't sure she had the emotional capacity to do it.

"You make a conscious decision about what you want in life, and you take one step toward it. Then another. You've said you want to be in love, to be married and have a family. You want a lifelong companion. A soul mate."

Yes. More than anything. But did Juliet really understand what they were talking about here?

"I want *him* like crazy," she said, smiling through her tears. "But then, when it starts to happen…"

Juliet waited.

"Well, if I don't do it, I might lose him," she whispered.

More silence.

"I feel so trapped. What I most want, I *don't* want. Which means either I'll never have what I desire most in life, a soul mate, a husband and family—or I live a life I can't stand, giving myself sexually without out sexual feelings."

"There's another option here."

Leslie peered at her counselor, the small Christmas tree in the background, almost hoping…

"You could talk to him about all this."

Her stomach fell.

"No." She stood up, grabbing her purse. "Absolutely not. Out of the question." The door was directly in front of her.

"So often, the right partner is a bridge to the final phase of healing."

Stopping, her back to Juliet, Leslie said, "I cannot tell him."

"Then maybe he isn't the right one."

Maybe not. Just maybe damn well not. Because Kip Webster was the last person she was ever going to tell about her past. If she did, she'd never be able to keep her deepest secret from him. And that was something she'd take to her grave. Leslie shut the door quietly behind her.

CHAPTER FOURTEEN

CLARA'S ARRIVAL late Saturday morning changed everything yet again. Loading his makeshift new family into the car to go to and pick up Leslie's mother at the airport, Kip had caught a glimpse of himself, as if from outside and above, and hadn't even recognized the man he'd seen. For a second he'd been tempted to tell Leslie to go by herself, to pull out his personal address book and find someone to spend the day with.

Someone impermanent.

And then Jonathan had called out to him to hurry and that was exactly what he'd done. What he'd wanted to do. Whether he recognized himself or not.

By evening, Clara, who was staying with them for the couple of days it would take to get her utilities and phone hooked up, had taken over the household. At least on the surface.

Kip had an idea that Clara would only be successful insofar as Leslie allowed her to be. Cal's little sister had grown up to be a woman who was strong in all the right ways. She was giving and compassionate, nurturing, but she had her boundaries and some- how managed to persuade others to honor them.

Her brother would be proud.

"Okay, you two, I have things under control here," Clara had said as they all finished the cabbage rolls she and Leslie had made for dinner. "Kayla's bath, then storytime and bed for these two—who, by the way, I'd like to spend some time with. Alone."

She grinned at her grandchildren, both of whom appeared to have taken to her immediately. The hand- held young learners' computer she'd brought for Jon- athan and the large wooden puzzles for Kayla hadn't hurt her cause any.

"The stores are open late," she'd continued, look- ing over her shoulder from the sink to the table, where Leslie had been wiping Kayla's face and hands before getting her down from her high chair. Kip had been sitting there, full and bemused and feeling like he should be doing something other than watching Jonathan play with the computer he'd hardly put down, except to watch the holiday video Clara had bought for them—one Leslie had apparently seen so many times she'd had it memorized. *Miracle on 34th Street,* the original version. It had been a first for Kip and the kids.

"You two should go out and do some Christmas shopping before everything's all picked over." Clara had come to the table to collect the last of the silverware.

Christmas shopping. Something else he'd never done. The thought appalled him. Intrigued him. Stumped him. His entire life he'd been envious of people who had those trees with all the presents underneath. He'd never once imagined being the person responsible for getting them there.

"How does one know what to buy?" he asked.

"You make a list," Leslie said, kissing the small cheek she'd just cleaned with a loud smack. Kayla returned the favor, adding a delighted giggle. "It's like any other project you take on—you get a sense of everything you need to do when you see it all down on paper."

Okay. He was certainly game to try. Christmas the way he'd done it all his life hadn't been much of a hit.

"WHAT DO YOU WANT for Christmas, son?" Kip knelt on the floor of Jonathan's room, while Leslie, who'd insisted asking was necessary, stood by.

The boy was sliding another disc into the slot on his new computer toy while Clara bathed Kayla.

"I dunno."

"Your aunt Leslie and I are going shopping tonight, so now's your chance to speak up."

Jonathan turned the device back on, his new program accompanied by a series of beeps and a tune about frogs and lily pads. "I dunno."

Another strike-out for Kip Webster, father extraordinaire.

He tried again. "If I were Santa Claus, what would you ask for?"

"I dunno."

If he heard one more "dunno," he was going to wash the kid's mouth out with soap. Well, not that, but he'd ban the words from Jonathan's vocabulary with some kind of stiff penalty attached.

Although what that would be he had no idea. Nothing mean. Who could be mean to a little guy who tried as hard to please as Jonathan did.

Kip's knee started to hurt—an old football injury—but he remained in place long enough to give Jonathan a chance to reconsider his lack of response. With his tongue sticking out of the side of his mouth, the boy pushed buttons. Beeps beeped and verses played.

And then there was a falling sound, followed by a computer-generated "game over." Jonathan didn't seem to mind that he'd lost.

He glanced up at Kip, over at Leslie, and back to Kip.

"Are you gonna get married?"

"Me?" He asked to buy himself time. *Of course you, idiot. Who else would he be talking to when he's staring straight at you?*

He stared back at the boy. It was becoming painfully clear that he needed a crash course in answering the awkward questions kids could ask.

"You and Aunt Leslie," Jonathan clarified.

Okay, well, *now* he felt better.

He could feel her standing there. *Don't look at her, man. Just don't look.*

"Uh…your aunt Leslie and I…haven't known each other very long and—"

"You knowed each other forever," the boy said, not quite glaring at him.

"Yes, well, that's true, but not as adults," he said. What he really wanted to do was draw Jonathan's attention back to the computer game that had been holding him in such thrall.

"Daddy's fun'ral was Thanksgiving."

"Yes." Kip nodded, completely unaware of how the switch in topic had come about, but not willing to question a fate that had smiled on him.

"You and Aunt Leslie knew each other then cuz you was together."

He'd work on the grammar later.

"Yes, we did." Did it give the child some comfort, knowing that? He'd like to think so. So much of the time, the little boy seemed emotionally self-sufficient. *Too* self-sufficient. Not that Kip was an expert on children, but he didn't think Jonathan's stoic attitude was natural.

"Them guys on the movie met at Thanksgiving, and Santa made them married for Christmas."

Leslie coughed behind him.

He'd walked right in to that one. He was going to have to be smarter to be Jonathan's father.

"Well…yes."

"I want Santa Claus to bring it to me and Kayla, too. 'Cept we don't need the house cuz we already got that—but maybe a baby brother would be okay…"

Kip had no idea how he replied. His thoughts were on fleeing. And as soon as he could, he did.

MIDNIGHT CAME AND WENT, and Kip still hadn't returned. Clara had long since gone to bed, telling Leslie not to worry about Kip Webster. He'd always known how to take care of himself, she said.

And he'd take care of Jonathan, too. Of that Clara was certain. She didn't mention the abandoned shopping plans. As was her way. She presented her opinion—but in the end, she was the master giver of space.

Glass of wine in hand, Leslie sat, dressed in the black slacks and red sweater she'd donned for shopping, in the armchair across from the couch where she and Kip had kissed that first night—and several nights since then. Christmas lights twinkled on the tree. Ornaments glistened. But she couldn't find the peace she craved.

Or the hope.

Her fingers found the red-and-black Sorrelli necklace at her throat, one of her favorites, antique gold with little chains of crystals hanging down. Tonight it seemed to be fresh out of strength to lend her.

Her arm, on the side of the chair, was bare except for the matching Sorrelli bracelet. She'd grown too warm and pushed up the sleeves of her sweater. She should be cold.

She couldn't sit on that sofa knowing that Kip was out making love with another woman. She'd spent her teen years dealing with this kind of pain. She would not spend her adult life the same way.

Taking a small sip, she set the glass down. It was still three-quarters full. She really didn't want any wine. She wasn't in the mood for the distraction—or the forgetfulness—it offered.

With Kip, sitting at home while he was out with another woman, would be a way of life. He was a playboy. Came by it naturally, both from his environment and maybe genetics, too, if that was possible.

The man loved women. And didn't see anything wrong with enjoying them.

It has nothing to do with the fact that you wouldn't even let him kiss your breasts.

Of course it does. A man with Kip's experience needs far more than chaste kisses.

So tonight he'd gone somewhere else, to someone else. He was probably with her right then, naked, his body sinking into hers.

Would he sigh when he found release? Or was he one of the noisy ones who grunted and punctuated everything with ah?

No, not Kip. He was definitely a sigher.

Sighing in some other woman's ear, holding her. Touching her naked body. Letting her touch his.

Giving her a part of himself he'd never given Leslie.

Taking from this unknown woman things he'd never had from Leslie. Knowing her better than he knew Leslie.

What was he like as a lover?

Did he pound in hard, or was he slow and gentle, aware of the body he was entering?

Stop it!

She was a grown woman now, not a messed-up teenager with a warped attitude toward sex and too much time on her hands. She—

The garage door opened.

She should go to bed. Grabbing her wine, Leslie stood and turned to the hall. And then sat down again. The last time she'd gone to bed before he was home, he'd come visiting. Clara was staying at her end of the house. She didn't want her mother knowing Kip was in her room.

She sipped her wine. Tensed at the thought that he might go straight on to bed, ignoring the lights in the living room. Ignoring her.

Tonight he'd no doubt been satiated. He sure as hell didn't need conversation with a neurotic frigid housemate, even if she *was* helping him raise his child. She closed her eyes against the vision of Kip and some beauty lying nude together, laughing. Maybe even at her?

Get a grip, woman. You don't need conversation

with him, either. A kiss or two would be nice. Wild sex you could enjoy would be great. Short of that, what you need is to finish your wine and get a good night's sleep. Tomorrow, you shop.

"I'm sorry."

Leslie's eyes flew open. Inside she jumped a mile high. But she managed to take a slow sip of wine and smile softly. "For what?"

"Running out like that."

"You don't have to apologize, Kip." She sounded calm. Just as she'd planned earlier in the evening when she'd still been more or less sane. Presenting to the world exactly the woman she wanted it to see. Confident. Unaffected. "Other than your responsibilities to Jonathan, you're a free man, and tonight his grandmother was caring for him. A perfect opportunity for you to go out."

He dropped down to the couch, his weariness making it a little difficult for Leslie to maintain her composure. The woman had been that good, huh? Good enough to wear out the legendary Kip Webster?

Or maybe he was losing stamina in his old age.

Of thirty-three.

Like hell. The man was in his prime.

She *had* to have been that good.

Damn her.

Who was she? Some bimbo he just met? A college professor with beauty as well as brains? A cover model?

"We were going shopping," he said.

Leslie frowned at him. He was actually planning to tell her about it? Surely even Kip couldn't be that dense.

It took her a full minute to realize he'd been talking about the two of them.

"We hadn't actually agreed on anything specific."

"I…it's just…"

"It's okay, Kip," she said, finding another smile and hoping she didn't need many more, since this one might've been her last. "What you're doing for Jonathan is incredible. You're one of the most decent men I've ever known. Don't go beating yourself up over something so unimportant. You obviously had another commitment…."

Now, if he wanted to hit himself a time or two for leaving Leslie's arms empty while he screwed another woman…

"You want to know how I spent the evening?"

No! Don't say a word. Leave me that, at least. "How?"

"Driving. Until I ran out of gas on some desert road and had to walk a mile and a half to find a gas station that was open."

Driving. Alone. Walking. Alone. Out of gas. "I thought your Expedition had a low fuel warning."

"It does."

"It didn't work?"

"No, it worked. I just didn't notice."

He'd been that distracted. And not by another woman. Leslie went for the bottle of wine she'd left in the refrigerator. She returned with an extra glass and sat beside him on the sofa. After handing him a full glass, she rubbed one hand down his back.

It wasn't like her to be that familiar. But at that moment, she couldn't *not* touch him. Offer him whatever comfort she could.

"You want to tell me about it?"

"All my life I've been a winner." He leaned forward, hands on his knees, staring into the glass he held. "Not because I'm anything special, but because I always saw life as a game and I always knew the rules, which meant my plays were right on target."

She would've described him that way once.

He turned his head and looked over at her, his brown eyes shadowed. "I don't know the rules anymore."

"Welcome to life."

He shook his head, setting the glass of wine next to the empty goblet she'd left earlier. "I mean it, Leslie," he said. "I'm completely unsure of myself."

"If this is a first, then your life truly has been blessed."

He met her eyes. "There've been times I haven't known what to do," he said slowly, as though measuring his words for accuracy. "But I can't remember a time when I felt so awkward. So ignorant."

"You're a very lucky man." Or maybe not.

According to Juliet, if you didn't falter, you didn't grow and learn.

"Me?" he said, nodding toward her. "Look at you.

You're at the top of your career at thirty. You own a great home. You're smart as a whip. You lose a business deal and have another half-dozen waiting in the wings. Your brother dies and leaves you a kid and you're an instant model mom. Nothing seems to throw you. It happens and you deal with it."

She didn't know what to say. He had it so wrong. But it sounded so good.

"You have a sense of what's right and wrong for you, and you stand by it."

"And you don't?"

"It sure as hell doesn't feel like it right now. Tonight, while I was driving, I actually thought about quitting the whole thing, signing Jonathan over to you and Clara and walking away."

And she'd thought he'd been having sex.

"Why didn't you?"

His gaze was intent as it held hers. "Because there was something here bringing me back."

"Because you have a sense of right and wrong, too, Kip Webster, and you love that boy, just as you loved my brother. You want to be there for him."

"Wanting it and knowing how are two different things."

"Oh, and is this perhaps borrowing trouble from the future?" she asked him, smiles flowing freely. Funny how a heavy heart could lighten so quickly.

"He asks so many questions that seem like life or death," he said, turning toward her as he took her hand between both of his. "I get the feeling that my answer is crucial—that it could affect the rest of his life. The most important game I've ever played and I've never even seen the rule book."

"You love that boy," Leslie said again, feeling as confident about this as Juliet had ever sounded about anything. "In this game, that *is* the rule book."

"Jonathan wasn't the only one bringing me back."

Leslie's aching heart soared. Her teenage, hurting self had just been vindicated. The worst evening of her adult life had been erased. Elation, sure and sweet, warmed her body, thrilling her with a well-being she'd never known before.

She held his gaze as long as she could.

And then she poured herself a second glass of wine. If she drank enough, could she be normal? Or at least be capable of pretending so well that he'd never know?

Wouldn't life with Kip be worth the pretending? Wouldn't it be better, so much better, than another evening like the one she'd just spent?

But wait—sleeping with him wouldn't guarantee that there'd be no more nights exactly like this one. Just because she'd brought him back tonight didn't mean he was hers forever. Kip wasn't a forever kind of guy.

He liked her. But he liked a lot of women.

And if he ever did go to another woman, *after* she'd slept with him, she'd suffer much more than she had tonight. She wouldn't be imagining what he was doing to that woman, she'd know.

And she'd know she hadn't been enough to keep him.

"Say something."

"Kiss me." *Let me lose myself for a few minutes in the only ecstasy I've ever known. I've had a hard night.*

Kip's mouth came closer, but it wasn't opening to cover hers. It was moving.

"Marry me."

Leslie took a sip of wine. A long sip. So long the glass was empty. And she felt sick.

"I've never seen anyone do that with a glass of wine before." Kip's tone was gentle, his expression a mixture of apprehension and humor. "Beer, whiskey, a bottle of water, I've seen. But wine…" Taking the glass out of her hand, he pulled her body into the crook of his arm, her head resting against his chest just beneath his chin.

"So…was that a yes?"

CHAPTER FIFTEEN

IN A DESPERATE ATTEMPT to stop a moment that had already happened, Leslie pressed her lips to his. She opened to him, using every wile she'd learned from her experience with the opposite sex—and tried for ten years to forget. Her lips softened, moving against his, her tongue tasting his lips, his tongue, the inside of his mouth. Slowly, seductively, she imitated the mating ritual, moving her tongue in and out of his mouth.

Having sex was an art she'd perfected with practice in college, learning the secrets of the trade. It was all about technique. Skill and confidence were the greatest sales tools. And she had a load of crap to sell.

Kip didn't seem to notice that her kisses were different. He didn't seem to notice that she hadn't answered his question.

Or was he taking her sudden sharing of her expertise as a *yes?*

His tongue darted inside her mouth, igniting that strange compulsion to spread her legs. She answered with a thrust of her own tongue—one that happened of its own accord, not calculation.

Leslie was having a hard time controlling her breathing.

As a matter of fact, she wasn't controlling it at all. Her breasts ached, her nipples tingled uncomfortably with the need to be touched by him, and her crotch was…getting wet.

With trembling hands, Kip lifted her sweater. She'd done that to him, made him need her so much he was shaking with it. The knowledge was heady, powerful.

Reacting, she pressed her breasts forward, eager for him to unclasp her bra, to free her swollen breasts, expose them to his view, his touch.

The clasp released. Her breasts were in plain view. Leslie's instincts turned on and she opened her eyes, to remind herself that this was different from anything that had come before.

Kip was gazing at her as though she were pure clean water in the desert and he was a man dying of thirst.

It was an expression, a desire, she'd seen before from a man she trusted. A man who couldn't control his own need for her even when it was sinful. Wrong.

Against the law.

A man who knew she'd give him what he wanted.

What she saw was not the man before her now but a man who'd been there, in her life. The only man who could possibly have stopped the events that had changed an innocent little girl into an experienced, tormented little girl. A girl who had nothing in common with the children who used to be her friends, but who'd learned how to keep secrets better than any of them.

"Les?" Kip was holding her away from him, staring at her with horror in his eyes.

She didn't blame him. Anytime she looked back, she was horrified, too.

Reaching to pull down her sweater, she was surprised to find that it was already pulled down, fully covering her. And her bra was fastened.

And she was still sitting just as she'd been when Kip had asked her to marry him. Her lips were dry. Untouched.

She hadn't kissed him. She'd imagined it all. The pretense. The passion.

Or rather, she'd been remembering both.

"Tell me what's wrong." He ran his hands over her shoulders, down her arms to take hold of her hands. "You're sweaty and shivering and your hands are freezing. I've been talking to you for five minutes and I swear you haven't heard a word I've said."

He'd been talking to her and she hadn't even known it.

"I CAN'T MARRY YOU."

Kip's hands dropped to the thighs of his black jeans. If he'd thought about it, he would've expected the rejection—knew of at least a dozen reasons marriage between them wasn't a good idea—but he had no explanation for the severity of her reaction to his impromptu suggestion. A laughing "no" would have sufficed.

"Why not?" he asked, hoping for some insight that would put him back on even ground, or at least ground that wasn't shifting so rapidly beneath him that it left him reeling. Something was going on. Something he didn't know about. Something bad.

Leslie shook her head, but her eyes were focused again, giving him a small measure of relief. If she wouldn't speak to him, how could he help her?

"You can trust me, Les. With whatever it is."

His words made her cry. Not exactly what he'd been hoping for. But then much of his life during these past weeks had gone that way.

"It's not a matter of trust," She said, obviously trying to quell the tears. "Or maybe it is. I'm aware that I have trust issues, as my counselor likes to put it."

She had issues. He wasn't the only person she couldn't trust. He slowed down—his mind, the beat of his heart, his breathing.

Amid the confusion, other things started to make a kind of sense. Whatever was wrong was far more serious than he'd suspected. Her rejection of his proposal wasn't because they'd only known each other as adults for a couple of weeks. Or because if the marriage failed the kids would be hurt. Or because she'd be committing herself to a man who'd never had a long-term monogamous relationship in his life.

He thought about her isolation and indepen-dence—hc'd been living in her house for weeks and she'd never received one personal phone call other than from her mother. And this, right after her brother had been killed. Surely friends should've been call-ing to see how she was.

He recalled her intensity at times he least expected it—like the previous Sunday night, when she'd been so upset over a conversation with Jonathan that had gone much better than he'd dared hope.

Her night-light.

Kip was afraid to ask himself what her secret might be. Afraid of what he might come up with. No point in wasting energy worrying about something that existed only in his mind. Particularly when his instincts told him he was going to need everything he had to help Leslie deal with reality—whatever that reality was.

But two things were clear. He wasn't going to let her sink back into her isolation.

And he had to go the distance with her.

SHE'D JUST GOTTEN UP to get a drink of water. Would never have dreamed of eavesdropping on Leslie and Kip—didn't want to be one of those nuisance moth-ers who didn't know when to back off. She'd seen what her maternal grandmother had done to her par-ents' marriage—judging her father, making sure her mother knew her opinions on his every action—driving a wedge so deeply between them that they fought constantly. And in the end, when her father gave her a mother an ultimatum—choose between the two of them—she'd taken a look at the options. Either live with a broken heart and guilt for turning her back on the woman who'd raised her, sacrificed to give her the life she'd never had, loved and protected her, or turn her back on the father of her children, the man she'd promised to honor and cherish until death, the love of her life. Apparently unable to accept either option, she'd created a third.

She'd taken her own life.

Clara hadn't issued any ultimatums when her own mother-in-law found her lacking in every way and didn't miss an opportunity to point that out to her adored only son. Instead, Clara had lived with the discomfort of never measuring up, the insecurity of not knowing if someday her husband would believe some slur of his mother's and walk out on them. In the end, he'd died, too. Racing home in the rain to make it to Calhoun's twelfth birthday party.

Yet now, as Clara stood at the window in the guest bedroom of her daughter's home, none of the past heartaches seemed to matter. Something was horribly wrong with Leslie. Her daughter. Heart of her heart. Her pride and joy and reason for living. Her hope. She was suffering, and Clara had known nothing about it.

What had happened to her daughter to make her

fall apart at a marriage proposal from a boy she'd loved all her life? When had it happened? How long had Leslie been suffering alone?

More importantly, what could she do about it?

LESLIE SHOPPED ALONE on Sunday. Clara and Kip were at the house with the kids. Thankful for once that her mother wasn't the kind who asked questions or got involved in her personal life, she'd been able to escape without explanation.

Just as she'd done the night before with Kip. Using the wine she'd gulped—and the lateness of the hour—as excuses, she'd managed to avoid any further discussion between them.

At least temporarily. Pulling into her driveway with a trunk full of shopping bags, Leslie felt her stomach tense and her head start to pound. The time away had been a distraction; it hadn't solved the problem.

Of course, ultimately, nothing would. She was what she was—a recovered victim. Nothing in this world would ever change the fact that she'd experienced things that had damaged her.

Leaving the bags in the car until she could get them into the house undetected, she unlocked the door from the garage into the back hall, listening for sounds of the children. Would they be having their afternoon snack in the kitchen? Or were they in the family room watching television?

She was met with total silence.

Maybe they were in the living room reading.

A quick check revealed nothing but furniture and a glowing Christmas tree. They wouldn't have gone anywhere with the tree plugged in. It was a fire hazard.

Frowning, she started down the hall to her part of the house. "Mom? Kip?"

Clara met her in the hall, her face creased with worry. "Jonathan's locked himself and Kayla in her bathroom," she said quickly. "I'm so sorry, honey. I was only in my room for a second. I left Kayla playing in her room. I thought Jonathan was with Kip."

Her first thought was the little metal key resting on the lintel above the door. It was her second thought as well. And her third.

"How long have they been in there?"

"Ten minutes or so."

The bathroom door was right ahead in the empty hall. Kayla was screaming. "Where's Kip?"

"At the door leading to the bathroom from Kayla's room. He's threatening Jonathan with all kinds of horrible fates and pounding at the pins in the door hinges."

Leslie hurried into the room. "Wait," she said to Kip, standing on tiptoe to reach the molding above the door.

"Your mother heard Jonathan tell Kayla he was sorry, but he had to do it," Kip was saying, his voice urgent, as she took down the key.

With one shove of the key, Leslie popped the lock and swung the door open. *He was sorry, but he had to do it,* was all she could hear as she rushed into the room, terrified she was going to find Kayla naked and praying she wasn't too late.

Kayla was still wearing the purple corduroy pants and matching white-and-purple flowered top Leslie had dressed her in that morning. Seeing nothing but that fully dressed form, Leslie swung her up, rushing her out of the room and down the hall to her own suite, where she locked the door behind her.

"It's okay, baby," she said, holding the toddler against her chest as she crooned. "My baby, it's okay, don't cry. I'm here. You're safe."

Falling to the side of the bed, Leslie rocked the child back and forth. "I'm here, little darling, don't cry."

Kayla's tears wet her neck, and the blouse she'd pulled on that morning. The baby grabbed her hair, yanking it from the barrette she'd used to keep it back. "Hay-er," she said with a hiccup that was followed by a dry sob.

"Yes, that's my hair," she said, reaching up to caress the top of Kayla's head.

"What?" she said aloud, drawing back enough to get a good look at the little girl. The braids she'd spent half an hour on that morning were nowhere to be seen.

"Where are your braids?" she asked the bewildered and still hiccupping child.

"Jon Jon, hay-er," she said again, her lower lip jutting out and trembling.

"He cut your hair?" she asked.

Kayla nodded, a big fat tear rolling down her baby cheek.

He'd cut her hair. It was a terrible thing. Atrocious. Punishable. They'd have to find out why.

He'd cut her hair. Trembling with relief, Leslie started to laugh. And to sob. Cal's son had only cut his sister's hair.

JONATHAN SAID HE'D DONE IT SO Kayla wouldn't look different from Leslie and Kip. They'd talked to him together, while Clara took Kayla for a walk around the block in her new stroller. Kip didn't think either one of them had said or done anything to help the situation.

Jonathan's young life had seen repeated occurrences of loss. His mother, his father, his nana. The little boy who needed more security at home than most had none.

"I hated punishing him," Leslie said Sunday evening. She sat beside Kip on the couch in the sitting room of his suite. The kids were asleep after a dinner of hamburgers and French fries—Kayla's choice—and Clara had gone out to a potluck function at the new church she planned to attend.

"A week without his computer will be no different than last week, when he didn't even have it yet," Kip told her, offering her the plate of cheese and crackers they'd prepared, in lieu of dinner, to go with the sodas he'd poured. She took the plate, selected a cracker and a piece of cheese, put them on the napkin in her lap. And studied them. The rose flowers in the paper matched her slacks. The background matched her blouse.

She needed to eat. Her stomach didn't seem to care.

"Still, it's hard to punish him for trying to protect his sister."

"There's a right way and wrong way of doing things," Kip told her. He'd been strangely unbending through the whole situation. "He has to learn that now."

Closing her eyes, leaning her head against the back of the couch, Leslie hoped that someday right would be easy.

"I ASKED to speak with you privately for a reason," Leslie said half an hour after she'd followed Kip down the hall to his suite. It was the first time she'd been there since he'd moved in.

She was fooling with her necklace again, something he'd noticed her doing a few other times. The day he'd gone to her office to tell her about Cal. At the law firm of her brother's attorney. The first night they'd talked.

"I assumed that," he said now, wishing he knew how to put her at ease. She'd declined his offer to get them some wine to go with the cheese and crackers they were having, not that he would've been able to drink much.

For the last hour, his stomach had been feeling the way it had before the All-American playoff game his senior year of high school—ever since she'd asked to put Jonathan down in her room. Then she'd picked up the baby monitor receiver, connecting her to Kayla's room, before leaving with Kip.

"I didn't want to take a chance that my mom would come home in the middle of things."

He'd assumed that, too. And knew better than to hope it was kisses Clara might've been interrupting. He was half expecting her to tell him to move out. And half expecting some rehearsed explanation for her odd reaction to his marriage proposal the night before.

He didn't know how he was going to get her to open up to him. He'd leave if she asked. And accept whatever reason she gave for not marrying him. But he couldn't just abandon her to whatever torture she was feeling.

"I…" She glanced down at her uneaten cracker. "This isn't easy for me."

"I understand."

She sent him a pointed glance. "No, Kip, I don't think you do," she said with uncharacteristic sharpness. "There's really no way you could."

He bowed his head once, silently, in acknowledgement—since he had only his own guesses as to what this was all about. And then he looked over at her, hiding nothing. "I want to."

She nodded, taking a sip of her cola. Her hand shook as she set it back on the table. "Frankly, I'm not even sure I'll be able to get through this...."

"Borrowing trouble from the future again, Sanderson?" It was probably an asshole thing to say—insensitive and inappropriate. Kip rubbed sweating hands along the legs of his khaki slacks. Swiping at a nonexistent speck on the chest of his black polo shirt.

"Just take it one step at a time, okay?" he said, glancing over at her hesitantly when she didn't respond. He was so afraid of screwing this up—of not being what she needed. But how the hell could he know what that was when he was running blind here?

Carefully folding the four corners of her napkin around a cheese-topped cracker, she nodded again. She didn't look up. Didn't do much but shudder for a moment or two. Kip waited.

"This afternoon, when I came home and found Jonathan in the bathroom, I learned something about myself."

Once again she'd caught him completely off guard. This was about Jonathan? Not about last night's proposal?

"What's that?"

"I'm not as healthy as I wanted to believe."

"Healthy how?"

"Mentally," she said, folding the napkin, unfolding it, refolding. "Emotionally."

When no response occurred to him, Kip remained silent, knowing that he was completely out of his element.

"The thing is," she said now, her words accompanied by a humorless chuckle, "I really had convinced myself that I had it all under control. That I'd done my job, dealt with my…issues, and other than one area that I'm still working on, was fine."

"You're one of the healthiest people I know," Kip said. "We all have crap to deal with, Les. Stuff from our pasts that screwed us up, even if it was only the fact that we had perfect parents, a perfect childhood and nothing in our adult lives will ever be as perfect."

Her lips trembled. "I put up a good front."

"Maybe," he acknowledged. "To some extent, everyone does. But I'm not talking about that. You're leagues ahead of many of us because you're aware of yourself." He had no idea where the words were coming from, but they seemed right. "You're strong enough to take an honest look at yourself, to see the good and the bad—and to try to fix what you don't like."

"I didn't have a choice," she replied in a voice that wasn't quite steady. "It was either do that—or lock myself up."

"Of course you had a choice." He should shut up and let her get on with whatever she had to say. "Les, I see people every day who've spent their whole lives blaming other people for what happens to them. Nothing is ever their fault. And if they believe that, they have no power to fix the things in their lives that they don't like."

She glanced up from the napkin and then back. The brief glimpse gave him very little to go on.

"I know what I'm talking about," he continued, despite that. "I don't blame others for what happens to me, but I've spent much of my life refusing to look at the things I don't like about me. With one exception. The time I listened to Cal about women."

Leslie crushed the napkin, cheese and cracker and all, in the palm of her hand.

"For the most part, the guy I was in high school is the guy sitting before you now. And that's because— to this point—I've done little to make him more."

Something stronger than cola would've been better. Anything to stifle words he hadn't even been conscious of thinking—yet *felt* clear to his core.

Leslie tried to smile at him. Her lips moved upward slightly, but did nothing to crack the stiffness of her expression. He wished she hadn't taken her hair down. Though normally he loved to see it wild and free, tonight it allowed her to hide from him.

And he was already in the dark.

CHAPTER SIXTEEN

JULIET MCDANIEL DIDN'T often indulge in flights of fancy. And she didn't buy into new-age philosophies, many of which, in her opinion, were a convenient excuse to relinquish accountability for individual actions and choices. If it was always about other people—their issues, their journeys, their realities—then it could never be about oneself.

She very rarely, however, ignored her intuition. And Sunday night it was prompting her to call a client at home. Something else she rarely did without predetermined instructions.

Leslie Sanderson had called her that afternoon. Her message had said only that she'd like to schedule an appointment for the following day. Nothing unusual about that right now. The call had been just like the other three she'd received from the woman who'd come to mean much more to her than a client. Leslie was an example of the human ability to heal—of the power of choice and openness to eradicate darkness. She was an inspiration to Juliet, who'd studied all the books, accepted most of the philoso-

phy, had practiced for years—and still hadn't understood what it was all about until Leslie Sanderson, a
twenty-year-old anorexic, had called and asked for
her help.

Listening to the computer generated voice of Leslie's home answering machine for the third time in
an hour, she hung up, trying Leslie's cell phone number again, just in case.

Getting no answer, she turned off her phone, lay
down, and willed herself to sleep. But not before
saying a prayer that the morning would find Leslie
alive—and in her office by noon.

Something had happened. Leslie needed help.
And Juliet was not about to let her down.

"I CAN'T FIND a way to begin."

The lost tone in Leslie's voice was too much for
Kip to tolerate without action. He moved across the
couch, taking her hand in his.

"Whenever you figure it out, I'll be right here."

She seemed to nod. Or else she was swaying to
some internal force. A couple of minutes later, she
started to cry. Kip held her hand. And waited.

When the tears turned to sobs, Kip still held her
hand. And waited. Some unknown instinct was guid-
ing him, and he gave himself over to whatever it was.
He sure as hell wouldn't have known what to do.

After awhile Leslie's sobs quieted. Other than an
occasional welling up, the tears stopped. But the

empty look on her face disturbed Kip more than anything that had gone on before.

"Thank you for being so patient," she murmured.

"I'm here because I want to be," Kip told her. "There's no need to thank me."

"It's just…well, when that happened with Jonathan today, I realized you're the one person I have to talk to about this."

"Okay."

"When it was just about the marriage proposal I wasn't going to."

So much for his assurances to himself, as he'd fallen asleep the night before, that Leslie would confide in him as soon as she'd had a chance to rest.

"But you're Jonathan's guardian, responsible for him and his well-being, and you have a right to know that I might not be good for him."

What? It took everything he had to keep his mouth shut.

"The reason I can't marry you, can't marry anyone, is because I'm frigid."

Kip cleared his throat. Kept his hand steady. He had to disagree with her. "What gives you that idea?"

"It's not an idea. It's just something I know."

"Leslie, are you forgetting who you're talking to?" he asked, willing her to look at him. She didn't. "I've kissed you, and let me assure you, there was nothing frigid about that."

"There was when you touched my breast."

The energy left his body. He had assumed she'd stopped so they didn't rush things. Didn't make mistakes. He'd never once considered...

Couldn't believe what she was implying.

"You didn't feel any desire at all when I touched you?"

"No, I felt some."

He'd thought so.

"And then it shuts off and I'm...repulsed."

Okay. So they had a bit of a problem. It wasn't insurmountable. "We'll go to a counselor," he told her, his mind racing, "get some help..."

"I've been seeing a counselor since I graduated from college."

This had been going on since college? And what did any of it have to do with Jonathan? "Why did you start seeing a counselor back then?" Seemed a good place to begin.

"Because I was so anorexic I couldn't find any professional clothes that fit me. They don't make many good-quality suits or professional styles smaller than zero."

He'd seen her at her graduation and hadn't noticed any excessive thinness, but then he hadn't seen her without her robe, either. She'd come to greet him and Cal and Clara in the stadium after the ceremony. He'd left before they all went out to dinner.

"So, why were you anorexic?"

He knew a little about the disease, but mostly that

it afflicted dancers and models. Not straight-A business majors.

"Ah, Kip." She glanced up at him, her eyes watery, as she squeezed his hand. "I really don't want to tell you this."

He had to know. "You said it has to do with Jonathan." Perhaps the reminder wasn't fair, but there were times you just made a move, rules or not.

She nodded. Stood, taking her cola with her. Leaning against the opposite wall, drink in both hands, she glanced over at him. "I lost my virginity when I was twelve."

Kip nodded. Sat, hands folded on his lap, waiting for words that would make sense. What he thought he'd heard couldn't possibly be correct.

"He…was someone…I trusted. Implicitly. When it started, I had no idea what was going to happen. I went along with it because he was older, an authority figure, someone I believed would want to take good care of me…."

Blood rushed through his veins. He could feel it filling his face. Leslie, the woman he'd known practically since she was born—sweet, innocent Leslie— was telling him something that could not be true.

Yet he knew she wouldn't lie to him. Not about this.

"He told me he loved me, in a special way, that made me the most important person in the world to him. He asked me if I loved him more than anyone else in the world, too."

Kip had known Leslie when she was twelve. Her wild curls had always been in pigtails. She'd had long gangly legs, never wore makeup and was the sweetest kid he'd ever known. She'd trailed along behind him whenever he was over, offering to help him with his science project when he'd had trouble getting things arranged artistically enough on the poster board. The end result had garnered him the highest grade in the class.

He hadn't been aware that she'd even been closely associated with a man, let alone spent enough time with him to...

"He told me that if I loved him, I'd let him see my breasts. They were just starting to develop and he said only the most special people in your life were supposed to see them. He wanted to be that special person."

No! The word screamed silently in his brain. Your mother was that person. Only your mother. He could feel tears deep inside him. He didn't know how he was going to just sit there. Who was it? A teacher? He'd have the bastard hanged.

Hands still folded on his lap, he held her gaze, didn't move.

"I felt really uncomfortable, and I told him that, but he promised me it would be okay. He said we were different—lucky that we loved each other like that. He said if I didn't, he'd have to go away and never come back."

Let him leave. Good God, please let the bastard leave. Before he sees anything. Touches anything. You're a child! A little girl! I knew you!!

I was right there.

And I never knew.

God, how could I not have known?

"When he asked me to take off my shirt, I did."

Heart pounding, Kip clenched his hands so tightly they hurt. His back and legs were soaked with sweat. But she continued to hold his gaze. And he sat. Unmoving.

Maybe it had been a neighbor. But who? He'd known them all. Couldn't imagine any of them committing such atrocities.

"At first, I thought that's all it was going to be. I told myself it wasn't so bad. Just letting him look at me. It was worth not losing him…."

Still she stared at him and it finally dawned on Kip that she wasn't holding his gaze at all. She wasn't even seeing him.

"Then he told me he was going to touch them. I asked him not to, but he said he had to. I was scared of that, but more scared to be alone. He'd convinced me he was all I had. That without him I'd have no protection. He convinced me no one was going to love me as much as he did. And he told me again how lucky we were to love each other so much."

Had it been a boy at school? A gang member, maybe? Someone who'd first frightened her to death, then promised to keep her safe? How could Cal have not known?

"He touched my nipples."

Kip needed to yell *stop*. But he knew she had to go on. She'd been carrying that memory around for far too long and shouldn't have to do it alone.

"They got hard and he told me that meant I wanted him to touch me that way."

The bastard. He was going to kill him. Leslie deserved to have him killed for what he'd done to her.

"He asked me to lie on the bed with him, just so he could hold me. He took off his shirt because he…he wanted to feel my nipples against his chest."

The cheese and crackers started to come back on him. Where was her mother when this was going on? Where were he and Cal?

How could this have happened to such a sweet girl, from a good family, in an upscale neighborhood where there was plenty of everything to provide a happy, secure childhood?

"I went to the bed with him, lay down with him and let him hold my chest to his. I thought we were going to sleep. And then I felt his hand slide under the waistband of my pants. He didn't talk to me anymore. He just…did things."

Kip couldn't imagine a torture horrible enough for the man. But he was trying anyway.

"He pulled my pants down. He opened my legs and touched me there. He put his finger inside me and started to move his body against me, breathing heavily. He told me I was a good girl. That he was going to take care of me forever. I started to cry when he took his pants off, but he told me he wanted to give me the most special part of himself and that he wouldn't ever give it to anyone else. He said I wouldn't have to worry about him leaving me like my daddy had. He promised he wouldn't hurt me."

The expression on Leslie's face never changed. Whatever hell was going on inside her, she was showing none of it.

"He kept touching me with his fingers and when he climbed on top of me and pushed inside, he was mostly right. It only hurt for a minute. And then…it didn't feel bad. He finished pretty fast."

Her chin puckered on that last word, and then tears filled her eyes.

"It was wrong but it felt good…."

She was dying. Right before his eyes. Feeling remorse for a crime against nature that was absolutely no fault of hers.

Kip stood, crossed the room in two steps, reaching for her. Leslie collapsed against him, her legs weak, and he wondered how she'd managed to stand without falling. Leading her to the couch, he helped her sit. Took her glass from her. Was relieved when she crossed her arms over her chest—as though she was emotionally healthy enough to be able to protect herself.

Whether or not the gesture signified anything of the kind didn't matter at that moment.

Sitting down close enough to tend to her if she needed it, Kip tried to keep some distance between them. He didn't want her to feel threatened. She was so precious to him he ached with it. Watching her there, closing herself off, he felt the tears rise up within him, fill his eyes, spill down his face.

And in that moment, everything that had been unclear to him his entire life became clear. Everything had led to this.

He was in love.

And he would spend the rest of his life doing whatever it took to honor that love. And Leslie.

"WHO WAS HE?"

Leslie sucked in air as Kip's words registered. They were the first touch of reality she'd felt in what seemed like years. She was sitting on his couch when the last thing she remembered was walking to the wall.

"What time is it?" she asked.

"Nine-thirty."

"Is Mom home?" She'd been due at nine.

He nodded. "I heard her come in a little while ago. Sounded like she walked to her room."

Tears drenched her eyes as she thought about the woman she adored—even though she still felt anger toward her for something Clara knew nothing about. Leslie had considered herself beyond all that. She thought she'd forgiven her mother for being human, realizing that Clara would never knowingly have hurt her. That, in fact, Clara would've given her life to spare her daughter and that she'd been the best mother she knew how to be.

Once the tears started again, they just kept coming—an unending well inside her, always present. So many of the books she'd studied said that shedding light on something horrible took away its power. But it felt as though the darkness had been illuminated so she could see the horror that much better—feel it that much more.

She'd brought hell to the surface, and now even the parts of her life that had escaped the past were tainted with it.

"I feel so dirty," she said, seeing no reason to pretend any differently.

"You look like an angel."

His voice sounded odd, and she almost believed him. But then, Kip had always been nice. Which was, she supposed, why she'd had such a crush on him all those years.

Besides, how could he know who she really was? *What* she was? He still had no idea. "It didn't happen just once."

"I wondered." He sounded sorry, not shocked. "How many times?"

Nice. He was a nice man who asked hard questions in a tone of voice that made her feel safe.

"From the time I was twelve until I was sixteen."

It sounded like he hissed. Or swore, maybe. She didn't have the energy to look at him. To feel what she'd feel if she saw his face. She just wanted to go to bed. To sleep forever.

She'd tried that once, too. But the over-the-counter sleeping pills hadn't been strong enough. Or she hadn't taken enough. She'd ended up with a bad case of nausea and diarrhea and a week-long headache.

"I never had an orgasm," she felt compelled to say. "But after that initial time, he never hurt me." The truth wasn't pretty. It just was.

"What happened when you asked him to stop?"

How had he known she had?

"Which time?"

"Any of them. All of them."

"He'd tell me again how special I was. How much he loved me. What a good girl I was. He told me that if it wasn't meant to be, I'd never be able to please him so completely. As I got older, he threatened me a time or two. He said he'd tell everyone it was my fault. That I seduced him. Sometimes he'd beg. One time, the last time, actually, he cried."

"Did you ever fight him?"

She shook her head, the shame overwhelming her again. She'd often wondered why she hadn't been stronger, hadn't tried harder to get away. Why had she always looked to others to save her? She'd relived it all, so many times, until she was no longer sure about any of it.

And, until she'd found Juliet and worked through the residual self-defeating behaviors, she'd destroyed herself with blame. Regret.

"The requests to stop were always before we got undressed. Once that happened, I'd already agreed to go along with things one more time."

"God, I'm sorry, Les. So sorry. You don't deserve this. Not *any* of it."

"He was good to me," she said. And then added, "It wasn't all horrible. Being with him made me feel safe. I was so afraid to lose him. I was weak."

"You were a *kid*. A kid without a father, Goddammit! He manipulated you! He abused you!"

"I knew it was wrong."

"He told you it was special, as though he was above the law, better than the law!"

"I could've told someone," she said. She and Juliet had discussed that part of it many times. Leslie still hadn't completely healed from the mistrust of self that had resulted.

"Why didn't you?"

Leslie felt the bitter laugh inside her, but was incapable of releasing it. "That's the sixty-four-million-dollar question, isn't it?"

"No," Kip said, facing her. But he didn't touch her. She'd noticed that since she'd told him her dirty little story he hadn't touched her once.

It didn't surprise her.

"I asked because I want to know every bit of the torment you remember from that time. I want to know because I don't want you to be alone with it ever again."

She began to cry. Where had he learned such beautiful words?

"I didn't tell…" She had to stop to breathe. To swallow. To find some numbness. "Because I didn't see the point. As far as I was concerned, the damage had already been done. I wasn't like any of the other kids anymore but as long as I kept quiet, nobody knew that but me."

"You and the bastard who was holding you hostage to his depraved urges."

"I also didn't tell," she continued as if he hadn't spoken, "because I didn't want him to get in to trouble. You see, Kip, even after all that, I still loved him. Other than that he did things to me, physically, that weren't right, he was very, very good to me—and I was scared to death to lose that. To lose *him*. Most of the time I really did believe he was all I had."

He grew deathly silent beside her, as though he wasn't even breathing. She wondered what he was thinking. What he was figuring out.

"Who was he, Les?" The words were quiet. Firm.

She had to tell him. She knew that. *It's what this is all about.* Jonathan. Kip. Her.

The end of eighteen years of silence.

"Calhoun."

CHAPTER SEVENTEEN

"THIS AFTERNOON, with Jonathan...I thought..."

Kip nodded. "I know." He'd spare her what he could. It was three o'clock in the morning; they were still on the settee in his room, drinking water from the bottles he'd collected when Leslie excused herself to the restroom an hour before.

"I'm afraid I shouldn't be around him," she said, her eyes tired and swollen as she looked over at him. "He's already facing such issues with prejudice and not fitting in—to the point that he's shaving his head and cutting his sister's hair—and I'm showing an even worse prejudice against him, tainting him with his father's brush."

Kip longed to pull her into his arms, to find a way to soothe her heart and mind. But he was hesitant to do anything that might not be good for her. First thing in the morning, he was going to make some calls. He had to know what he could do to help Leslie—and himself as well.

He'd never been so angry. If Calhoun Sanderson were alive, Kip would be hunting his sick ass down, and when he found him, he'd kick him in the balls until he suffocated. And then break his neck.

Prison be damned.

"You're Jonathan's family," he said, finding reservoirs inside himself he didn't know he possessed. "You're one of the few blood relations he has left. He needs you."

He needed her, too. He needed her forgiveness. He'd been there. He'd been Cal's best friend. He'd listened to Cal talk about sex. Women. One woman.

"He needs someone who'll help build his self-esteem, not doubt him."

He couldn't think about Cal. He'd barely made it to the bathroom in time to throw up when he'd first heard the truth. But he'd recovered. Leslie needed him right now. He'd find a way to live with himself later.

"You didn't doubt Jonathan," he told her, doing his best to communicate the love he felt with words and looks. It was all so new to him. The need to protect. Placing others before self. "You reacted based on traumatic past experience. And even then, you kept the reaction to yourself."

"If he'd known what I was thinking…"

"We all have thoughts we'd like not to have, Les," he told her, "The only thing that matters is what's in your heart. You know that. More than anything, Jonathan needs love and you have that to give him in abundance."

She still didn't seem convinced. "I need you to

promise me you'll be aware and that you'll protect him from me if you think my past is affecting him in any way."

And then something else occurred to him, a thought he might've had much sooner had he not been so caught up in horror.

"Is it hard for you, loving the kids, knowing who fathered them?"

Could a woman love the child of her rapist? A tough question he couldn't answer.

"No." She shook her head. Her smile was tired, but it was probably the first genuine smile she'd cracked all night. "In the first place, they're human beings, separate and apart from him," she said. "Just as I wouldn't care or not care for you based on the man your father was."

That made sense, logically, but the heart was pretty independent, making its own decisions that often had nothing to do with logic.

"Now that you know, does it change your feelings for Jonathan?"

"Of course not." *Of course not*. Thank God.

"And in the second place," Leslie said, the smile fading from her mouth but still warming her eyes. "I loved my brother, Kip. There was one part of him I hated, one weakness that nearly destroyed me, but it destroyed him, too, you know. Aside from that one thing, he was a wonderful man. Gentle, giving, selfless."

"I've begun to see that I made a life out of being

selfish, Leslie, and yet I would *never* have dreamed of taking for myself something that would irrevocably damage another person."

"I don't think he saw it that way," she said softly. "I think he really loved me…that way. To him, it was only society's laws that were the problem."

"What about the fact that you didn't want it?"

"As he kept reminding me, he was in a position to know better than I did what was good for me in other aspects of my life. It carried over."

"You can't convince me that what he did wasn't one of the worst betrayals a man can commit. One of the worst *crimes*."

"It was." She leaned her head against the couch, her eyes half closed. "But if I'm going to heal, I have to understand what really happened. And part of the understanding is to realize that life wasn't fair to Cal, either."

He might be sick again. Just hearing her defend the bastard set him off. He held back the tears and wondered if there'd ever again be a time when they weren't there.

"He was grieving, too, Kip. Not only did he lose the father he adored, his mentor, his safety and security, but he was given responsibility far beyond what was fair to a boy his age. He was a child himself, being asked to raise a child."

"So he shouldn't be held accountable?" Kip asked, some of the anger that corroded his soul spilling over in spite of his attempts to spare her. "The prisons are full of guys who had it rough, Leslie. I had it rough. So did you. How does that give any of us the right to commit horrendous acts?"

"It doesn't."

Kip silently cursed himself as her tears welled up again.

"Cal paid for what he did, Kip. Not in the eyes of the law, but I believe it ate at him every day of his life. That first year, after he left for college and I finally had some time away from him, I grew stronger. Once I saw for myself that I could make it without him, that I didn't need him as much as he'd convinced me I did, I made up my mind that he'd never again see me alone. When he was home on break, I slept over at a friend's, or at least that's what I said. Most times I checked into a motel. And once I left for college, I never went home again anytime he was there. You see, in the end, he lost the one thing he loved most in the world. Me. I haven't seen him since he attended my college graduation."

He'd wondered. Was slightly mollified, but only because it meant Leslie hadn't had to deal with the bastard or suffer through any further encounters with him.

"Abby certainly saw something in him," she was saying. "And you know he suffered, too, that he was sorry, based on what Jim had to say about their relationship. Abby helped him find forgiveness for the parts of himself he hated." She looked at him now. "Everyone has weaknesses." Leslie's gaze was compelling, but he wasn't anywhere close to seeing his best friend as anything other than vile. "Cal's weakness was unacceptable," she continued, "but that still doesn't define the whole person he was, just as you aren't judged only by your weaknesses."

In this case, the weakness did define the man. Everything he'd known Calhoun Sanderson to be had simply burned up, as if it had never existed. Only ashes remained.

Cal had committed one of the greatest sins known to man and that was all he was.

"MARRY ME."

Four o'clock had come and gone. They both had to be in the shower by five-thirty to make it to work on time. Leslie had shown no signs of leaving his room. And as long as she stayed, Kip was going to be there for her. He didn't want her to leave. Ever.

"I can't marry you." The rejection was accompanied by a sad smile, almost as though she was humoring him. "And you don't really want me to," she said, reaching over to run a hand along his arm.

Her touch was magic. Comfort and hope and a heady anticipation of the unknown. Those sensations infiltrated his skin.

He grabbed her hand, threaded his fingers through hers. "Yes, actually I do."

Leslie shook her head, still wearing that weary, knowing smile. "You just think that right now because it's been a grueling night and we're exhausted. You're feeling sorry for me. And that's no reason to get married."

"I asked you to marry me before I knew any of this."

"But when Jonathan mentioned us getting married you ran off because it was all too much for you."

"I didn't run off. I went for a drive. I'm not used to being out of my element, and I needed some time alone with myself." He squeezed her hand lightly. "I had a lot of time to think that night and no matter how I looked at things, I kept coming right back to wanting to marry you."

"Kip, I'm frigid. I can't marry anyone."

"We can get help."

"And there are no guarantees it'll work."

"Marriage is about far more than sex, Les." He hadn't ever expected to propose marriage; even less would he have imagined meaning the words he'd just said.

Yet they rang completely true to him.

Leslie shook her head. "You love women. You enjoy sex. I care about you too much to tie you to a possible lifetime without it. And I also care about you too much to stand by while you get it elsewhere."

Okay, obviously they had to deal with this little issue so they could go on to bigger topics—like the rest of their lives. Kip took her hand, brought it slowly toward his crotch, giving her a chance to pull away at any time. On the contrary, she seemed quite willing to go where he led.

And then, with her hand in place, he released his hold on her. "What do you feel?" It took every bit of control he had to appear unaffected by that touch.

Her hand began to move, slowly, up and down. He let his mind go, aware only of Leslie. Not of the horrible truths he had to learn to live with. That would come later.

And when his body hardened, growing with an intensity that would soon have a life of its own, he stopped her.

Frowning, hand back in her lap, she silently questioned him.

"There are many ways to give and take pleasure, Les," he said softly, enjoying the slight flush on cheeks that had been far too white. "Let's give that concern a rest, huh?"

MONDAY PASSED IN A BLUR as she tried to stay focused enough to get through the hours until bedtime. In the end, she'd left Kip's room with the question of marriage still hanging between them.

But it was overshadowed by her bigger concern that, when she saw him again after he'd had a chance to think about what she'd told him, things would be different. He'd look at her differently. Or worse, not look directly at her at all.

"You know how it is," she said to Juliet at noon. "When people know you've gone through some horrific event, they start to see you as defined by the event, instead of as a three-dimensional person."

"When they don't know you well, that happens," Juliet had said. "People can only define you as far as they know you."

She'd finally told her counselor that the abuser in her past had been her brother. Juliet hadn't seemed all that surprised. Which didn't really surprise Leslie. Juliet had suggested that perhaps they ought to meet a few more times to talk about it, not the physical abuse but the abuse of trust.

Juliet had also given her some reading to do on reintroducing the body to desire after abuse. And given her the name of someone to call if she wanted to talk about what she'd read. She seemed to think that if Leslie was willing to try some of the suggestions in the book, she'd be pleased with the results. She said that Leslie had been preparing for this next step and her time had come.

Leslie didn't know about that. What she knew was that she would always have a guide and a dear friend in Juliet McDaniel. The counselor's relief when she'd opened her door to Leslie at noon had warmed her heart in a way she'd never forget.

ON TUESDAY, upon seeing Nancy's reminder of a black-tie charity function she'd agreed to attend that evening, she called Kip in his new presidential office at SI and asked if he'd be able to get home in time to be her date for the event.

She'd escaped to her bed the moment she got home the night before and still hadn't seen him since leaving his suite early Monday morning.

"It's fine if you'd rather not," she said quickly, not wanting him to read anything more than a last-minute need for an escort into the request. "I can ask Mom. I thought maybe you'd rather not bother with putting Kayla to bed." There, that sounded unromantic enough.

Sort of. If you considered talking to the man whose proposal you'd turned down about putting the kids to bed in the house you shared as unromantic. Leslie had always seen domestic affairs as the height of romance. But then, her list was lacking most people's top choice—sex.

Although when Kip had put her hand on his crotch the other night, asking her what she'd felt, her heart and belly had both flip-flopped. As they had every time she'd thought of that moment since.

Which was far more often than she'd ever admit.

"I'd be honored to go with you." Kip's reply interrupted her mental ramblings. "What time should I be ready?"

Agreeing to meet him in the kitchen at six, Leslie disconnected and pushed speed dial to reach her mother and ask her once again to watch Kayla and Jonathan. She was afraid that otherwise she'd change her mind and send word that she was ill to the client who'd invited her to attend tonight's function.

Judging by the weight in the pit of her stomach, she wouldn't have been far off in saying so.

KIP'S SUSPICION that he had it bad was confirmed Tuesday evening, dancing with Leslie. He considered himself lucky just to be holding her close. The sensations that swept through him as her body swayed against his almost had him acting like an inexperienced schoolboy attending his first prom instead of the man of vast experience that he was. The slinky, long black halter dress she was wearing didn't help matters. Nor did the fact that the silk trim on his tux slid so easily against her back, making it far too convenient for his hand to end up at the curve of her buttocks.

Had she shown any sign of displeasure, he would have removed his hand instantly. But she'd stepped closer to him, fitting her thigh between his as they finished the slow song that was playing and stayed on the floor for another.

She was safe here; he understood that. Fully dressed, with an audience of people who both liked and respected her. In this room she was not a young victim of sibling incest. She was Leslie Sanderson, Finance Analyst, and soon-to-be partner at one of the most prestigious privately owned brokerages in the country.

And if this was the extent of the intimacy she could freely offer, Kip still considered himself lucky to be the recipient.

That scared the hell out of him.

THE COOL NIGHT AIR DRIFTED over Leslie's skin as they walked to the parking garage in downtown Phoenix where they'd left Kip's Expedition. Buildings and lamp posts glittered with Christmas lights, which illuminated the shiny metallic ribbons on the wreaths adorning many of the streetlights. Ah, Christmas. A time of hope. Of possibility.

So why did she feel as though, for her, the season was already over? She'd come full circle. Had faced the past. Been offered the culmination of all of her deepest dreams. And she'd turned it down.

"There were a lot of beautiful women there tonight." No point in rubbing her own nose in it, but she was facing reality these days, not running from it.

"I didn't notice," Kip said, nice as always. His arm brushed hers as they stepped down to cross the street.

The downtown consisted of little but offices and the bars and restaurants that served the professionals who worked in them. It virtually closed down at night, unless there was a baseball or basketball game in the nearby stadiums, or a function at the symphony hall. Tonight there were still some partygoers making their way slowly along the streets.

"It's hard to believe it's only five days until Christmas."

"There've been a lot of distractions this year."

Yes, well, she didn't really want to talk about that.

Face burning, she wished for the thousandth time that she hadn't told Kip about Cal. To hell with Juliet's assertion that she'd taken a major step forward. She felt like she'd slipped back eighteen years. Only this time, she had to look at the past with hindsight gained from the present, from an adult perspective.

"I found Jonathan's backpack tonight when I was putting his dirty clothes in the hamper in his closet," he told her suddenly.

"Oh, good." She knew he'd been concerned that the bag—one of the last gifts from his father—had been lost in the move.

"It was packed with clothes, including underwear and pajamas, some toothpaste but no brush, several individual packages of teddy grahams—"

"I'd bought a box of them, but couldn't find them," Leslie interrupted, frowning.

"…and the copy of *Huckleberry Finn* we just finished reading."

"So he packed recently."

"Uh-huh."

"You think he's going to run away?" The thought made her ill with fear. Her sensitive little redheaded champion out on the streets alone?

"I'm sure he's thinking about it."

She stopped abruptly, digging in her small black evening bag for the flip phone she'd never been anywhere without since Kayla came into her life. "How can you be so calm?" she asked Kip. "We have to tell my mother, warn her to keep a close watch—"

"I've already done that," Kip said. "I also talked to Jonathan about it."

Sliding the phone back in her purse, she resumed walking, her heels clicking against the cement sidewalk. "What did he say?"

"That he was just cleaning up his room like his grandma told him to."

"He lied to you."

A man dressed in baggy pants and a torn and dirty beige shirt, sitting against a lamppost on the corner, held out a shaky hand. Kip reached into his pocket, pulling out a handful of change, and dropped it into the other man's hand.

"Not for long," Kip said. "As soon as I started praising him for minding his grandmother, he broke down and told me he might have to leave for Kayla's sake."

Her breath caught in her throat, Leslie managed to ask, "Why?" Only one more block to go and they'd be at the car where she could sit, closing her eyes to shut out a world that had grown confusing and difficult.

"Because she'd pass as white and if we didn't have him causing us so much trouble maybe we'd keep her and get married and be a real family. That's what he said."

"He's not causing any trouble." Other than the haircutting, none at all. In a few short weeks, the little boy was already a vital part of her life.

"I told him that, but he's still blaming himself."

"It's a common symptom arising from childhood loss," she said, half to herself.

She almost missed Kip's pointed look. And brushed off his silent intimation that she should look a little closer to home.

"What are we going to do?" she asked instead.

"Get married."

Leslie didn't even bother to respond. He was beginning to sound like a broken record when they needed to find real answers.

She'd never realized Kip Webster had such a small repertoire of ideas.

CHAPTER EIGHTEEN

HE WAS LOSING HER.

Kip might only know what he'd been able to learn in two days regarding victims of sibling incest and its aftermath, but he knew women, and the walls Leslie was building around her heart, around her life and her secret, were growing higher by the second.

Almost at the house, he pulled off the road onto a dirt track that would eventually lead up the mountain to someone's home. Tonight it was deserted, private, and it offered the same gorgeous views of the city that Leslie had from her living room.

"Why are we stopping?"

Putting the SUV in park, he turned off the ignition, still not quite used to the fact that he didn't need the heat on in the middle of December. "We have to talk," he said, facing her. The moon up in the mountains was full and brighter than the lights that shone from the city below them, illuminating her face as brightly as any lamp might have done.

"We have a perfectly good house where we can talk."

"With a child near your room, another near mine, and your mother staying with us. We covered some pretty hard issues the other night, Les, and I'm not prepared to slide backward. I'm serious about wanting us to get married."

She shook her head, face impassive. "Give it up, Kip, we aren't getting married. But we should go home and sleep. We both have to work tomorrow."

He turned, an arm on the steering wheel, cautioning himself even as he spoke. "You've known me most of my life, so you know by now that I don't suffer from any great lack of confidence."

"That's certainly true." The dry comment was accompanied by a grin that hid more than it revealed. She was still Leslie Sanderson, Finance Analyst. Somehow he had to find Leslie Sanderson, person. He needed her to trust him, and according to the counselor he'd seen the day before and all the reading he'd done since, trust was going to be the hardest thing for her to recover.

"You also know I'm not easily daunted when I set my sights on something."

She wasn't as quick with a comeback to that one. As a matter of fact, she said nothing at all.

"I'm not out to conquer you, Les, or to force you into anything you don't want. I'm not out to convince you what's best for you. What I want is for you to give me a chance—" She started to interrupt and he shook his head. "Just hear me out. And by that I mean really listen, okay?"

Her lips trembled as she watched him in the moonlight and he had a feeling she knew exactly what he was asking. He wanted her to hear, honestly and completely and without defensiveness, what he had to say. "I'll try."

Kip opened his mouth, relieved to have made it over the first hurdle, and found he couldn't speak. The remainder of his life might very well rest on the next few moments.

"I want to marry you because I love you." They were the hardest words he'd ever said. And in the end, because their truth was stronger than his fear, they were also the easiest. "I've held back that part of myself for thirty-three years," he went on, so stunned at what he was doing, light-headed with the relief surging through him, that he told her exactly what he was thinking. "It's like I've spent that time preparing myself for when it would finally happen."

"You're confusing sympathy—probably with a bit of misplaced guilt because you didn't know about Cal all those years—for love."

"I'm confusing nothing," he told her, his expression grim. "And you said you'd really listen."

Her chin sank to her chest, in acknowledgment he thought, of his point. And then she raised it again, as though inviting him to go on.

"I've had everything else, Les. Every kind of man-woman relationship it's possible to have, within the bounds of law and human decency, of course. I've had one-night stands, six-month stands, ten-minute stands. I've dated older women, younger women, women who were friends first and I've been friends with women after we decided to stop being sexually involved. I've been with whores and virgins and even a lesbian once."

She blinked at that—as he'd meant her to do. If he had to shock her, he would. Maybe he'd crossed over the fair-play line again, but he was playing for keeps.

"I've been with women I was so attracted to I could hardly think of anything else. I've had girl-friends who made me laugh, girlfriends whose conversation was stimulating, some who lived wild and adventurous lives and others who liked staying home in the evenings. There've been tall ones and short ones, skinny ones and even a few who weren't so skinny. For the most part, I enjoyed all of them."

She swallowed and her eye twitched, but she said nothing. She turned her head away, gazing out toward the world of twinkling lights beneath them. All the lives down there. All the stories and passion and pain.

Life was confusing.

"The reason I'm telling you about these women is not to brag or because I think it in any way adds to my character, or desirability, or worth. It's because if there's one area in which I *do* know what I'm talking about, it's my relationships with and feelings for women."

She was sitting there so proud and determined,

and he wanted so badly to hold her until all the pain inside her melted away.

"And what I know is this. In all my experience, I've never before felt, even remotely, what I feel when I'm with you. Or when I think about you. Or when I'm walking down the street and someone inadvertently reminds me of you. My feelings go far beyond sex, though I do find you incredibly attractive and think about making love to you. I look forward to coming home at night to hear about your day. The thought of you in the kitchen gets me out of bed in the morning. And the thought of what Cal did to you…" He stopped, waited, and then tried again. "It breaks…my…heart." The tears he'd held in check until then choked him, but Kip didn't stop. "In this very short time with you, I've discovered a deeper meaning to life and I don't even want to contemplate living without that."

Crossing her arms over her chest, she asked, "And when did you discover this love, before or after I told you about the incest?"

"I think it began when you heard that my father had forgotten my birthday and you cried."

"It was your sixteenth," she said, her voice softening ever so slightly.

"He made up for it with one hell of a nice sports car."

"It didn't make up for anything." She'd turned her head, was looking at him.

"No, it didn't. Nothing did until I found you again."

"Even if it's true, Kip, even if you do love me, it's too late."

He'd played his only ace and after more than half an hour of trying to convince her, he was about to lose the hand, anyway.

The dirt path was barren, as was the road that led to it. In all the time they'd been there, not another car had gone by.

"It's not too late. It's never too late."

"Maybe not for people like you," she said. "You, Kip, you fall down, you get back up and brush off your knees and figure it was all part of the game, to use that analogy you like. Me, I fall down, I get back up but my knees are scraped and bleeding and I can't walk as fast and I don't want to slow down the whole team."

"Tell me something." Kip forced himself to see this through. "Do you love me?"

"Kip! I...there's no point in—"

"You said you'd had a crush on me for years," he persisted. "And you responded to my kisses when, according to you, you've never felt even a hint of desire before...."

"Yes, but..."

"Do you love me, Les?" Everything was on the line now.

"I..."

She tried to look away, but he wouldn't let her

escape, willing her eyes to stay locked with his. "Do you?"

"Yes."

"IT DOESN'T CHANGE ANYTHING."

She was just wrong about that. Kip was still sitting in the car. So was she. Fifteen minutes had passed since her confession, and he still faced seemingly insurmountable barriers, but he had the determination necessary to overcome them.

"Les, we love each other. That's all we need to get through whatever lies ahead."

She shook her head, not budging at all. "Love is not selfish, Kip. What kind of love would it be if I allowed it to trap you?"

"It won't trap me."

"We don't know that."

"I do."

"I know one thing very clearly," she said, sitting up straight, staring down at the valley. "I know I cannot trust myself to make it work. I know I can try, and that it *might* be okay. I also know that I'm sensitive and weak, and when I'm really up against the wall, I might not come through."

He wanted to tell her she was being ridiculous, but one of the things he'd learned in the past two days was that victims of abuse spent plenty of time beating themselves up. What they needed from their partners was building up.

"I saw a counselor yesterday."

That got her attention.

"He said that as the partner of a survivor of sexual abuse, I'd need to have more compassion, patience, understanding and love than I thought it was possible to have."

Her eyes filled, but Kip continued anyway, although his voice softened. "When he said that, Les, it was like some kind of confirmation clicked on inside me, validating all the new and strange feelings I've been experiencing since the day I walked into your office.

"What it all means is that you don't *have* to come through. If it takes this whole lifetime and beyond, I have the patience to stand beside you, to be the one you know will be there when you fall."

"But don't you see?" she said, tears streaming down her face now. "Cal loved me and I loved him, but my love made me weak and I didn't take care of him! I didn't make him get help. I didn't fight him. In the end, I didn't even tell him no!"

He understood, sort of, the self-blame she inflicted. She'd been seriously injured at the most impressionable time of her life; she held herself responsible because she hadn't known how to save herself. The natural order of things had gone sickeningly awry, yet rather than blame fate or her mother or Calhoun, it was as though she'd determined that *she* was at fault for not being able to prevent those atrocities. And because of that, even now, all these years later, she didn't quite trust herself to be there for anyone, not even a child. She'd been betrayed by the very person meant to provide safety and security when *she* was a child, but she also believed she'd betrayed herself.

At least that was his take on it. But what did he know?

He was so much in love he felt her pain as his own.

"Love does not make you responsible for another person's choices, Les." He spoke from his heart, not relying on the books or the counselor. "We're all here to either make it or fail, as the case may be. Love is our chance to get the strength and support we need to make it, but if we choose poorly, we can ruin that chance."

He'd been willing to adore his father if the old man had given him even a hint that his affection would be welcome—if he'd spent even one evening a month at home with him.

He was afraid of her silence, afraid the fear inside her, the inability to trust, was working up some new case against him.

"What about Kayla?" he finally asked.

"What about her?"

"You love her."

"I know."

"And you haven't turned your back on her, in spite of your fear that your love makes you weak. On the contrary, you've agreed to be her primary caregiver, her protector and provider."

"I had to," she whispered, but he could see his words had hit a mark. "She's a vulnerable little girl and I know what can happen…"

"Yes, you do, honey," he said softly, reaching to brush a curl back from her cheek, not because it was out of place, but because he needed to touch her. "And since you know what can happen, you've got a better chance of protecting her."

"Oh, Kip," she said, trembling as her tears wet the hand that still rested against her cheek. She turned her face into his palm. "You're confusing me."

"Good."

"It's not good. You keep talking about how aware I am, and how I make choices based on that, yet when I try to do so, you keep stopping me."

"I didn't say all those choices were the best ones," he told her, trying to smile, to ease her way. "Don't you see, Les," he said, completely serious again almost immediately. "You're already trusting yourself to love a helpless little girl, and that's a much greater risk than loving an adult who can look out for himself."

"Did I say—ever—that I trusted myself to raise Kayla?" she asked, her eyes wide and glinting with self-reproach. "I don't. I worry every day that I might screw up and that she'll end up being hurt by something I did or didn't do."

"And isn't that how it is for every parent?" he

asked. "You're the one who told me that. There hasn't been a day since I picked up Jonathan from his nana's house that I don't worry about the very same thing. We do our best, Les. It's all we can do."

She didn't speak for a long time. Kip let the silence, the peace of the night, wash over him.

"It's another reason to marry me, though," he dropped softly into the night air.

"What is?" There was no defensiveness left in her tone. Just a hint of resignation and a whole lot of uncertainty.

"Our doubts about being good parents. Everyone knows two heads are better than one. Checks and balances and all that. If you marry me, you save Jonathan from me—a guy who knows absolutely nothing about being a parent, not having had a working example to learn from. And you gain a reasonably intelligent, rational adult as a safeguard in case you miss some important clue with Kayla."

She didn't say no. Kip noticed that immediately.

"Kayla and Jonathan, particularly Jonathan at the moment, need a solid home, Les. They need security. Permanence. Think how much easier it'll be for them to bring friends home if they can show a well-kept house with a mom and a dad who are married, as opposed to trying to explain separate parents, separate suites, for separate kids all in the same house."

"I hate how cruel kids can be," Les said. "Most of them are just repeating things they've heard from their parents and don't even know how harmful their words can be."

"Jonathan's lost so much, Les. And he might be a little guy, but smart as he is, he's figured out that if we're married, it'd be a lot harder for either of us to pack up and leave him."

"Okay."

"What?" Mouth open, Kip reeled his mind back from the next stage of his campaign and stared at her.

"Okay," she repeated.

"Okay, what?"

"Okay, I'll marry you."

HE WANTED TO DO IT as quickly as possible—a trip to Las Vegas the next day. His second suggestion had been in front of a justice of the peace three days later. Leslie had always dreamed of a church wedding. And wanted to buy time to talk herself out of this madness, or at least have time to change her mind if she found she couldn't go through with it.

They compromised with a plan to speak to Clara in the morning and see how quickly her mother could arrange a church wedding—preferably, according to Kip, before the end of the year. That gave them a week and four days. Her mother was good, but maybe not that good.

And then, apparently having accomplished what he'd set out to accomplish, Kip fell silent.

Leslie had no idea what to do next. Sitting in Kip's

Expedition, she stared out into the night, at the view she'd spent half a million dollars to have at her disposal every night. Generally, the city lights brought her a sense of peace as she imagined sitcom-type families at home, having their dinners, helping children with homework, giving baths, going to school events. And later, when all was quiet, holding each other in sleep.

Tonight she wondered if there was even one house out there with people who actually lived that way. Or did each and every one of those lights represent broken dreams and lost hopes?

Marrying Kip. It was what she'd dreamed of all her life. And now she didn't know if she could accept it....

Kip shifted beside her and she turned to find him watching her, the warmth of his eyes obvious in the moonlight.

How could she look into those eyes, feel his heat, his kindness, the safety he offered and think that life was cruel?

"Are you ready to go home?"

"No." She'd have to go to her room and pretend to sleep or risk waking her mother. Both seemed beyond her at the moment.

But he was probably exhausted. "We can leave, if you need to," she offered. She'd go for a walk. She paid a hefty homeowners' fee each month to ensure the neighborhood's security.

And the bobcat that had been spotted in the area was much less of a threat than the emotions racing through her, the thoughts and memories attacking her mind.

"I'd like to suggest something, but I want you to be completely honest with me if you aren't up for it."

She couldn't tell what he was thinking, but it sounded ominous. Still, it was probably better than lying sleepless in her bed. Or facing her mother. "Okay."

"The counselor said something yesterday…"

Leslie's stomach tightened all over again. Was this the way it was going to be now? Her past being brought up at any time? She'd never considered that, once the secret was no longer just hers, she'd given up control of it. She'd given up her ability to turn off the volume, to close her eyes to the memories. She'd lost her ability to pretend.

Many days, that was all that had saved her.

"…I've done a lot of reading, and…"

Kip appeared to be struggling for words. Unusual. Intriguing. And very sweet. In spite of the topic.

"What?" she said, finding a new understanding in that second. She'd had eighteen years to accept what had happened, to come to terms with the fact that the brother she'd adored had been so ill. Kip had had less than forty-eight hours.

"Over and over, I came across the observation that abuse, especially incest, retards the development of the victim beyond the age when the abuse occurred."

"I don't know many twelve-year-olds with a seven-figure yearly income."

"Usually only certain areas of development are affected."

She had no idea where he was going with this.

"Healing can come if the person's able to go back and relive those years, or aspects of them, whether through writing, or art, or actual experiences they missed out on."

"I tried journaling. I developed writer's cramp and a huge paranoia that someone was going to read what I was writing. And I'm no good at art, so the blotches of color on my canvas were a waste of paint."

"I'd like to try an experiment."

"Okay." She'd tried hypnosis, acupuncture, herbal remedies—not to mention any number of self-defeating behaviors—to find some peace. At this point she was open to just about anything.

Kip touched her lower lip, then met her eyes again. If he didn't stop, he might distract her from the idea of healing.

And they already knew that his kisses led straight to failure.

Right now, though, she was willing to accept the consequences. He hadn't kissed her since Friday and, despite everything, she'd gotten used to it.

"I'd like to take you back to a first date we might have had, Les," he said, his voice, his expression, completely serious. "You said you had a crush on me."

Her throat was thick. "I did. All through junior high and high school."

Surprise lit his eyes. "That long? How could I not have known?"

"You were too busy getting laid," she told him, allowing only a hint of the pain that had caused her to come through.

"I was a fool."

No. He'd been a relatively healthy teenage football star. While she'd been busy hiding dark and shameful secrets.

"So…we're going to rewrite history, just for tonight," he said. "If you're game."

"If you can rewrite history for even five seconds, I'm game," she told him, trying to find the woman who'd been at that party tonight. And finding, instead, the young girl who'd once lived for the dream that Kip Webster would ask her to the prom. That child had honestly believed she would die happy if only she could have that one night.

"We're at the ice-skating pond at the corner of Alum Creek Drive," he said, naming a spot in Columbus a lot of the kids had gone to when they were young. "I'm holding your hand and all your friends are envious."

Kip took her hand and Leslie closed her eyes, imagining the cold biting her nose and toes, her skates gliding on the ice, the breeze rushing by her, the sound of other kids' voices, yelling to each other.

A girl screamed as she went down on the ice. Her friends laughed. There was a firepit over where they changed their shoes. She could smell it. And hot dogs cooking.

"It's the Halloween party of my freshman year," she told Kip. "Everyone was there that night...."

CHAPTER NINETEEN

OVER THE NEXT HOUR Kip took Leslie on two years' worth of dates. They held hands, he put his arm around her, they laughed. He kissed her good-night, quick chaste pecks. And that was all.

And then he was home from college her junior year. They were in his father's camper truck parked on a deserted dirt road out at Alum creek. She'd heard of that place. Almost everyone who was going steady went there.

She'd never been.

The sound of the Expedition's door opening returned Leslie abruptly, disappointingly, to the present. Kip hurried around to the back, opened the hatch, grabbed something that he shoved under his arm. Then he pushed a button and the seats in the back went down.

Her heart started to beat rapidly.

Next he was at the side door behind his seat, pulling a lever, lowering that seat. And then he was directly behind her, moving quickly through the dark night, his footsteps mere whispers against the desert floor.

She'd heard stories about things that had happened out at Alum creek. Crazy wonderful stories about skyrockets and bliss. About love and tenderness and…

He was climbing in behind her, spreading a quilt. And back out again, getting closer.

Her door opened and Kip's hand appeared. "Come and lie down with me, Les," he said softly. "We won't do anything you don't want to do. Just lie with me."

Her stomach got that excited roller-coaster feeling and she felt hot. She really wanted to do as he asked. So she took his hand, slid out of her seat and, completely disregarding the expensive gown she was wearing, hitched it up and climbed inside the cocoon he'd made for them.

Kip's kisses started out different from the way Leslie remembered. More hesitant, less passionate. While she appreciated what he was doing, *loved* what he was doing, she hungered for the more mature expression she'd grown addicted to over the past weeks. But he wouldn't let her rush him, kept breaking off to talk to her about inane things like wedding rings and Christmas presents and eggnog.

And then he'd kiss her again, propped up on his elbow beside her in the back of the car, leaning over to gently caress her lips with his. By the time his tongue entered her mouth fully, engaging her in a ritual she'd come to know with him, her lower body was actually aching with a feeling she didn't recognize at all.

Could this be the beginning of an orgasm?

Dare she hope?

Kip smoothly unhooked the halter strap around her neck but didn't pull the material down. Aware of what he was doing, she thought briefly that this was when it would end, disappointed because she wasn't ready to stop, and then his tongue distracted her again, advancing and then retreating.

He was driving her crazy.

In some foggy area of her brain, she supposed that was his plan. Kip Webster was very good at what he did.

His lips left her mouth, trailing over her chin, her jaw, until he reached her neck. Delicious goose bumps spread all over her body and she arched toward him. She was a teenager, curious, in love, trusting. While his arms supported her back, his tongue trailed a course from her throat down to her chest, leaving soft kisses in its wake.

She moaned. And felt more pressure deep in her belly when Kip moaned, too. Imagine, Leslie Sanderson out with Kip Webster, and him wanting her so badly he groaned with it. The thought was heady. The knowledge that Kip's arms were around her in real life, his lips against her skin, made her feel lightheaded and giddy.

She felt her dress slip down further, knew where he was going. She wondered how the cool air would feel on her naked breast. And waited for the wet and satisfying sensation of his mouth against her nipple. It was hard and throbbing with the need to be touched by him, by his mouth.

So slowly she wondered if she'd go insane with waiting, he made his way closer and closer to her craving tip, exposing more and more of her skin along the way. The hardness of the car beneath her hips was a strange comfort to her, reminding her that she was a teenager. Safe. She cried out when Kip's tongue first touched her nipple. Reaching upward, she pressed against him, feeling vitally alive, physically aware as she'd never been before.

"You are so beautiful. Like silk. What you do to me, woman."

Kip's voice. Thank God it was Kip's voice. She was glad of the reminder. Wanted to remember always that she was with Kip. Only Kip.

The relief of that brought tears to her throat. And an awareness of the reason for those tears. Another voice, telling her how special she was. Words she needed desperately to hear—but hearing them in a way that was all wrong. Right and wrong, so messed up and confused.

His mouth moved to her other breast and because it had been aching, too, she offered it, waiting for the sweet relief. She felt the tug, gentle and warm. The softness of his tongue.

And more tears. Why couldn't *this* have come first? Why couldn't *this* be the only memory?

Leslie tried not to give in. She tried to sing a song in her head. To count percentages on a deal she was putting together. Anything not to go back, to feel Cal, or maybe worse, not to feel anything at all.

Kip's hand slid down to her thigh, moving up beneath her dress to the panties that were still wet with a desire gone cold. His pants were unzipped. Had she done that or had he? She could feel him against her leg through the cotton of his briefs.

And shot up. "No!" she screamed, covering her ears with her hands, shaking her head back and forth. "No! No! Stop it! Please stop it!"

"Ssshhh." The voice was soft, reassuring, but too male.

"Get away from me! Please get away…" She was crying, trembling, aware somehow that she was falling apart, and yet completely unable to stop herself.

"It's okay, honey, it's just me, and you're the boss here. Always. I'm zipping up my pants, now, see?"

Out of morbid curiosity, she looked. And was a little calmed when she saw that he was doing exactly what he'd said.

"You unzipped them, did you know that?" he asked her almost conversationally.

His easy tone prompted an answer. She shook her head. She hadn't known.

"I want to tie this up for you, okay?" he asked her.

Like a helpless child, she nodded.

"There, is that better?"

She nodded again. Tired, foggy-headed, unable to figure out what she wanted.

Or what scared her most. The feelings Kip had raised in her that she couldn't assuage, or the ones she'd raised in herself that prevented a normal life.

"You aren't angry?" She felt stupid, sitting there, a grown woman in a silk gown, her hair falling out of the updo she'd arranged with such care earlier that evening.

"Of course I'm not angry." His tone was gentle, as was the hand that smoothed the hair off her forehead. "It was good, wasn't it?"

"Are you crazy?" Leslie cried. "I freaked."

"But you liked it at first, Les, I could tell."

She had. She wasn't going to deny that. "But what good is it if I can't go through with it?"

"You're only seventeen, remember?" he asked. "You probably won't be ready to go all the way until you're at least twenty."

She shook her head, not so sure he wasn't the crazy one. "You're nuts, you know that?"

"What I know is that you were getting close to an orgasm," he said, embarrassing her with his frankness. Which was hard to believe considering the shameful and dirty things he knew about her.

"Admit it, you were," he said, a tender smile on his lips.

"Okay, yes, I was, dammit. And I wanted it so badly, Kip! What if there's something wrong with me? What if I just can't get there?"

"You can."

"How do you know?"

"I know female bodies," he told her without bravado. "Yours is ready and waiting for you to let it happen."

"You really think so?"

"I'm sure of it."

"I wish I had your confidence," she said dryly, wishing…she didn't know for what.

"Can you handle one more experiment?" he asked.

"Can *you* handle a crazy lunatic on your hands?"

"If she's you, always."

"Okay." She had no idea what he had in mind, but at the moment, she didn't care. He was Kip. She trusted him. And if anyone could help her, she realized it was him.

Not because Juliet had told her so. Not because the books gave her clues. But because her heart just knew.

"Let's move to the front seat," Kip said, surprising her. And perhaps disappointing her a bit. She'd thought for a second there that he had another miracle idea up his sleeve, one that might actually get her where they both needed her to be.

But she did as she was told, staring out at the city lights as she waited for him to come around the car to his seat beside her.

"Okay," he said, leaning over her to pull at the lever that adjusted her seat, tilting it back. Then he put an arm around her shoulders. "I want you to close your eyes and relax. The next few minutes are just about you, Les. Your pleasure. Nothing else. The entire universe is asleep except for you and me and I exist only to please you."

She grinned. "Careful, Webster, you might create a monster," she said, but she closed her eyes and tried to pretend she wasn't nervous.

"Relax," he said, running a hand lightly along her thigh. He caressed her belly, her thighs, reminding her to relax, that this was her time and that he was there only to give her whatever she wanted. He talked to her about how smart she was, how much her business sense impressed him. He loved her chocolate pixies and the fact that she was more apt to laugh than cry over spilled milk. He found her patience with Kayla's temper tantrums amazing.

And then he stopped talking. His hand grew more bold, but no less gentle, finding its way beneath the skirt of her gown, moving in circles around her skin as he gradually climbed higher. Leslie had never experienced anything like it. He'd seduced her with his words, his unselfishness, until she was actually *feeling* special.

And he'd seduced her with the idea that a moment existed purely for her pleasure. Leslie wasn't sure she could pull off that particular fantasy. Personal, physical pleasure wasn't something she'd ever concentrated on before. Wasn't sure she knew how. But for Kip she was willing to try anything.

And she wanted to try for herself.

The warmth of his hand was fully under her dress now and Leslie let her legs fall open just enough to let him reach her inner thigh. He touched her there, massaging lightly for a while, and then, accidentally or so it seemed, his knuckles touched her crotch.

He hadn't meant to. At least not yet. She was sure of that. But she'd liked it.

"Do you want me touch you here?" He brushed her again.

Her breathless "Yes!" came before she'd even had a chance to think about his question.

And what a wonderful *yes* it was. Powerful. She'd been given the choice.

She'd tell him to stop, too, just as soon as she had to.

Until then, and because this was only for her pleasure, because she was perfectly safe, and because she was damned curious, she spread her legs a little further, making his job a little easier. The first deliberate touch of his fingers against her femininity sent shock waves right through her.

"You liked that?" he asked her, placing soft kisses along her temple.

Sliding down further in the seat, Leslie spread her legs wider, nodding. She didn't open her eyes, couldn't. She was too caught up in the strange and wonderful world he was showing her. It would end, and when it did, she'd have to come back to herself.

"Let yourself feel the pleasure, honey." His words continued the enchantment. "You're allowed to feel this."

She believed him. And cried out when his fingers slid beneath the silk of her panties and touched her. He didn't slide inside as she'd expected—and feared—he would, figuring that was when it would end.

Instead he touched her further, rubbing softly at first and then progressively harder, faster.

"That…feels…so…goooood…." The voice didn't sound like hers. It was husky. Knowing. "Oh, Kip…" She had one knee against the door of the car, the other against the console. She felt herself heading someplace, reaching for something she didn't recognize at all.

"Ahhh," she cried out, finding the top of the precipice and diving off into splendor so complete her entire body rocked with it. It felt good. She felt so good. In love. Euphoric. Like she could do anything.

Spasm after spasm pulsed inside her and she swore she saw stars. And when they faded, she was overcome with such peace she thought she really had died and found paradise.

Except this was better, because if she'd died, she'd have had to leave Kip. She threw her arms around him, still reveling in sensation.

"Thank you."

"Ah, darling, you have no idea what you've given

me," he said. There was an odd note in his voice, and she opened her eyes to see tears on his cheeks.

"The physical act of sex is nothing but body parts performing actions," he told her, his eyes slightly wide as though he'd just discovered this. "It's the total giving of heart and soul that turns it into lovemaking."

She reached up, running her fingers through his short hair. "You've done this hundreds of times," she reminded him, always needing to be aware, to be honest. At least with herself.

"Strange as this is going to sound to you, I've just made love for the first time in my life."

"You didn't even get to do—well, you know… anything."

"Ironic, isn't it?" he said, still looking bemused as he grinned at her. "All that experience and it took you to show me what it's all about."

They had a long road ahead of them. Leslie didn't kid herself about that. It might be years—or never—before she could take Kip into her body and ride with him to the ecstasy she'd just experienced. But the thought didn't hurt her as it once had.

For some women, heaven was orgasm. For some it was ice cream. For Leslie Sanderson, heaven was having finally found her soul mate.

EPILOGUE

"THERE'S ONE MORE PRESENT, Kip! See, there's one more!" Jonathan, hopping from foot to foot in his race-car pajamas, pointed under the lighted Christmas tree about half past six on Christmas morning. He'd woken them at five with his squeals that Santa had come. Surprising herself, Leslie hadn't felt the least bit embarrassed to be caught sleeping in a man's arms.

"I see it, son. Why don't you get it out for me?" Kip asked, his expression rather serious for a man who'd spent the past hour playing Santa Claus for a couple of excited children. Santa Claus in hastily donned gray sweats and a white T-shirt. She could get very used to that version.

"Careful!" Clara said, looking peaceful in her cream quilted robe. Sitting in an armchair, her opened gifts stacked around her, she was sipping the coffee Leslie had just brought in. "Don't let the tree tip over on him!"

With a hand raised toward the trunk of the tree, Kip waited for the boy to scoot under it and back out, a small gold-foil-wrapped box in his hand.

"Mow! Mow!" Kayla sang, dancing around her pile of loot. She stopped, glanced down at the electronic color game Santa had brought her, and stooped to turn it on.

"Here it is!" Jonathan held up the box.

Kip took the box, and, recognizing the size, Leslie held her breath. "It says here it's for your aunt Leslie," he said.

Her gaze flew to his as Kip handed the box back to the child. Kip had already given her the complete Sorrelli Crystal Ice collection to wear for their wedding later in the week.

Eyes locked with Kip's, she took the box, opened it, and then glanced down. Inside the black box, nestled in a bed of black velvet, was the most stunning heart-shaped diamond ring she'd ever seen.

"Seems Sorrelli doesn't make rings." Kip was still standing by the tree. "But I figure you don't need the magic from the crystals as much anymore."

Giving him the box as he approached, holding out the ring finger of her left hand, she had to agree with him.

"WAIT!" Jonathan cried from his knees as, ten minutes later, Leslie stood to go and make breakfast. The boy had been snapping together the easy tracks from an oversize electric train set Santa had brought him. He looked up at Kip, who nodded.

"We have one more present for you," he told Leslie.

"I've had far too many already," she said, so filled with blessings she wasn't sure she had room for more.

"I think you want this one," Clara said, moving over to perch on the edge of the couch. "Sit."

Leslie tucked the violet silk robe beneath her and sat.

"Kayla, come here," Jonathan said in an urgent whisper, as though Leslie wasn't meant to hear. He grabbed his sister's hand, yanking her away from the wooden puzzle she'd just dumped on the floor.

Kip followed right behind the kids as they walked toward her.

"Okay, Kayla," Jonathan said importantly. "Who's that?" He pointed right at her.

"Ma ma ma ma ma!" the little girl said, then toddled back to her puzzle. At least that was where Leslie thought she'd gone. She couldn't quite see through the haze of tears.

Her mother was right. She wanted this gift. And would spend the rest of her life living up to it.

She'd waited thirty years, hoping, always hoping. Today, the promise of Christmas had been kept in full.

THE RED ROCK MOUNTAINS of Sedona were one of a kind, miraculous, a colorful marvel to all who saw them, and the perfect setting for a wedding that would transform the impossible into reality. A damaged woman had found healing and happiness, orphan children were being given parents and a real family for the first time in their lives, and a man who'd been satisfied to settle for affection had found true love. They were a pretty fair match for the amber and maroon cliffs that rose above the city and touched the sky.

An hour before the outdoor wedding was due to begin, during that week between Christmas and New Years, that time between ending and beginning, Clara found her daughter in the hotel suite where she'd spent the night. Leslie had just finished her shower and slipped into the toweling robe she'd wear until it was time to put on the beautiful beaded gown her mother had found for her. And then altered to fit Leslie's thinner waist.

"Mom, is something wrong?" Leslie asked, when she saw her mother standing outside her door without Kayla. Clara was dressed in the long, snug-fitting violet gown Leslie had picked for her, and she looked every bit as lovely and elegant as Leslie had known she would.

"Can I come in?"

"What is it?" Leslie asked. Surely she wasn't going to lose everything now, not when she was so close to having it all. "Is it Kayla?"

"No, dear," Clara said, tucking a strand of Leslie's flyaway hair behind her ear. Kip had asked her to wear it down today. "She's with Ada."

The older woman had arrived in Phoenix the morning before and had driven up to Sedona with them. She'd hand-carried the papers from Ohio that had made Kayla and Jonathan officially Leslie and Kip's children.

"Is it Kip? Is he here?"

"Of course he's here," Clara said, pulling Leslie down on the bed beside her. "You think anything's going to keep that man away from you and the kids?"

She hadn't thought so, but this believing thing was hard work.

"I came because I wanted to talk to you," Clara said. "I want to make certain that you're really happy."

"Oh, Mom, of course I am!" Leslie almost laughed at the irony. Might have if she hadn't been afraid she'd cry instead. For thirty years she'd been waiting for her mother to ask that question. To ask any really personal question. And now, when Leslie had finally found her way alone, Clara was there.

"All I ever wanted was to be a good mother," she said, and Leslie's heart missed a beat. Did Clara know something, after all? Could her mother possibly have been aware and done nothing?

Leslie didn't want to think so. Couldn't bear to think so. *Didn't* think so. Clara would never knowingly have allowed Leslie to be hurt. She knew that from the depths of her heart.

And with that knowing came the peace and forgiveness she'd been struggling to find for years. Her mind had accepted the truth years ago. Today, her heart had.

"You *were* a good mother," she said, happy tears in her eyes as she said the words, free at last.

"I have a confession to make." Clara looked down, her cheeks flushing.

"What?"

"I overheard you and Kip the night he asked you to marry him."

She almost asked which night. But didn't want to give that much away.

"You told him you couldn't," Clara continued. "It was so clear that you'd been hurt, baby," Clara said, trying to restrain a sob. "Badly hurt. And I didn't know anything about it."

Thank God for that. Knowing would have killed Clara. And for no gain. Her mother couldn't have taken back what Cal had done, couldn't possibly have erased the memory, for any of them.

"I was always trying so hard not to repeat what my grandmother had done to my mother," she said, her eyes creased with pain. "And what your grandmother did to your father and me…"

"I know, Mom, it's okay. I always knew you loved me," Leslie told her mother. "Girls get hurt, Mom. Heartache's part of growing up. And they sure don't run to their mothers about it all the time."

"I suppose not."

"Kip is the man of my dreams, Mom. Surely you know that."

Clara grinned then, the lines of concern in her face disappearing. "I wish I knew more about your life, sweetie," she said, touching Leslie's cheek. "I wish we'd shared more."

"It's not too late to start," Leslie said, her heart bursting with happiness. It might have taken her all these years to find herself, but the life she was discovering was turning out to be worth the effort.

"I don't want to intrude."

"Mom, let's make a deal," Leslie said softly. "You ask all you want, and if it ever becomes a problem, I'll tell you."

"You promise?" Clara asked.

"Yes."

"And I promise I'll listen when you do," Clara said, standing.

Leslie stood with her mother, opening her heart completely as the older woman wrapped her in her arms. She figured, based on Kip's retarded-growth theory, that she'd just about caught up with herself.

THE CEREMONY WASN'T LONG, but every single word was significant. Leslie held Kip's hand and then, when it was over and they were pronounced husband and wife, she took one of Kayla's hands, as well. Kip, with Jonathan on his other side, escorted his family down the aisle between the dozen or so folding chairs. They'd been set up on the mountain outside town.

There were only a few guests, as Leslie had requested. The moment was too personal, too intimate; she didn't want to be conscious of onlookers.

But they were having a huge party on New Year's Eve for much of Columbus and Phoenix combined it seemed. They'd had to reserve half the rooms at the Phoenix South Mountain resort. Kip's friends from Ann Arbor would be joining them, too.

But for today, it was just her small family. Plus Ada, and Nancy. And of course, Juliet. Kip had met Leslie's counselor the week before, and it had been a mutual admiration party all around.

"Leslie, can I see you for a minute?" Ada asked, pulling Leslie aside after the lunch they'd had in a private room at one of Sedona's plushest resorts.

"Of course," she said, always conscious that her children had been Ada's children first. They'd already made arrangements for Ada to spend a couple of weeks with them in February.

"Cal asked me to give you this," the old woman said as soon as they were out of sight.

"He asked you? When?"

"The night before he left on that climbing trip."

"What is it?"

The woman shrugged. "He didn't tell me that. Just said I was to keep it and if'n you and Kip Webster ever got married, I was to give it to you."

Leslie thanked her, shoved the envelope into the white clutch she'd bought to go with her wedding gown, and promptly forgot about it. Cal no longer had power over her.

She found the letter again later that evening, in her hotel room with Kip, when she was transferring her things to the bag she was taking on her honeymoon. Kip had rented a villa for the two of them on the island of Capri, off the coast of Italy. Clara would be bringing the kids and joining them for a fortnight in Sorrento the following week.

The envelope she'd forgotten about earlier burned her fingers. A month ago, two weeks ago, she'd have hidden it away, feared it, until it drove her to open it. And then only when she was alone.

Tonight she turned, handed it to Kip. "Ada brought this. She says it's from Cal."

Watching her, Kip opened the envelope, cringing when Cal's handwriting became visible. He fell to the end of the bed, and Leslie dropped down beside him as, together, they read her brother's last communication.

Leslie and Kip,
Other than my sweet Abby, you two are the people dearest to me. I am leaving in the morning for the final adventure of my life. I will climb nearly to the top of one of my favorite mountains in Colorado, and then I will slip, get

tangled in my rope and fall. The thought brings me peace—something I've been without for most of my years.

There is no place for me in this life. I cannot stand to live with myself since losing Abby. Before I knew her, I didn't know what forgiveness and acceptance felt like, but now that I've had it, I find I can't live without it. I also find I can't live in the same world as my precious little Kayla. I am afraid for her, afraid of myself around her. I choose to die rather than risk hurting her as I hurt the only other little girl in my life, a child I adored as much as I adore Kayla.

That child was you, Les. I cannot stand the fact that I have ruined your chance at happiness. I know you've always loved Kip. And I know that you, Kip, are the only man I've ever known, who is worthy of my little sister. If anyone can help Les find happiness, it will be you. If anyone can help her find peace after living with a demon all those years, it will be you. You saw good in me, too, which is something I've never understood.

Kip, my friend, all you ever wanted was a family of your own, and a love that is real and deep. Leslie can give that to you. I am leaving the two of you my children because there's no one else I trust them to, but also because this is the only way I know to bring the two of you together—to break through the barriers and let you find each other.

If it's meant to be.

If it doesn't happen, you will never receive this letter, as I don't want to force my thoughts and desires on either of you. I've already done far too much of that.

I have no excuses to offer. Only this. I have been sorry with every breath I've taken for the past eighteen years.

Dear, sweet Les, I am so sorry.

The letter was signed simply *Calhoun.*

The piece of paper drifted to the floor as Leslie started to cry and Kip, with intense and very mixed emotions about his old friend, reached for her.

"I love you, Les."

"Even if I still love him? The person he was despite what he did to me…"

It wasn't as hard for him to understand as he might have thought. If Calhoun Sanderson were alive, Kip would do all he could to see him prosecuted to the fullest extent of the law. He'd see him sent to prison for the maximum sentence allowed by law, take his daughter away, have him registered as a sex offender. He'd never forgive or condone the horrible crime Calhoun had committed repeatedly for more than four years, regardless of the good the man had done. But he was no longer feeling murderous.

"Especially then," he told Leslie now. "That has nothing to do with Calhoun or what he did, Les, it's about you and your heart. You see the best in people. You look for good in a world where it's so easy to focus on the bad. And you find it—and show it to the rest of us."

She glanced up at him through her tears, so beautiful his heart ached. "You think so?"

"I know so."

"Do I show good to you, Kip?"

"Particularly to me, honey, because I know how hard you had to look to find it."

Her lips trembled, but her smile was bright. "Never that hard, even back then," she said. "Because right beside Cal, there was always you."

Pulling her close to his heart, Kip lay down with her, finding a release, a peace and euphoria far greater than any orgasm he'd ever known as she rested her head against his chest and fell asleep.

It wasn't a traditional wedding night. But it was perfect.

HARLEQUIN *Super*ROMANCE®

HOMETOWN
★ U.S.A. ★

An Unlikely Match
by Cynthia Thomason

Harlequin Superromance #1312
On sale June 2005

She's the mayor of Heron Point. He's an
uptight security expert. When Jack Hogan
tells Claire Betancourt that her little town
of artisans and free spirits has a security
problem, sparks fly! Then her daughter goes
missing, and Claire knows that Jack is the
man to bring her safely home.

Available wherever
Harlequin books are sold.

If you enjoyed what you just read,
then we've got an offer you can't resist!

Take 2 bestselling
love stories FREE!
Plus get a FREE surprise gift!

Clip this page and mail it to Harlequin Reader Service®

IN U.S.A.
3010 Walden Ave.
P.O. Box 1867
Buffalo, N.Y. 14240-1867

IN CANADA
P.O. Box 609
Fort Erie, Ontario
L2A 5X3

YES! Please send me 2 free Harlequin Superromance® novels and my free surprise gift. After receiving them, if I don't wish to receive anymore, I can return the shipping statement marked cancel. If I don't cancel, I will receive 6 brand-new novels every month, before they're available in stores. In the U.S.A., bill me at the bargain price of $4.69 plus 25¢ shipping and handling per book and applicable sales tax, if any*. In Canada, bill me at the bargain price of $5.24 plus 25¢ shipping and handling per book and applicable taxes**. That's the complete price, and a savings of at least 10% off the cover prices—what a great deal! I understand that accepting the 2 free books and gift places me under no obligation ever to buy any books. I can always return a shipment and cancel at any time. Even if I never buy another book from Harlequin, the 2 free books and gift are mine to keep forever.

135 HDN DZ7W
336 HDN DZ7X

Name	(PLEASE PRINT)
Address	Apt.#
City	State/Prov. Zip/Postal Code

Not valid to current Harlequin Superromance® subscribers.

Want to try two free books from another series?
Call 1-800-873-8635 or visit www.morefreebooks.com.

* Terms and prices subject to change without notice. Sales tax applicable in N.Y.
** Canadian residents will be charged applicable provincial taxes and GST.
  All orders subject to approval. Offer limited to one per household.
  ® are registered trademarks owned and used by the trademark owner and or its licensee.

SUP04R   ©2004 Harlequin Enterprises Limited

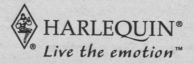

*Super*ROMANCE®

COMING NEXT MONTH